Mean Cuisine

by

Wendy W. Webb

A Beluga Stein Mystery, Book Two

Cover Art by *Kristian Norris*

The Wild Rose Press, Inc.
PO Box 708
Adams Basin, NY 14410-0708
Visit us at www.thewildrosepress.com

Publishing History
First Edition, 2025
Trade Paperback ISBN 978-1-5092-5927-4
Digital ISBN 978-1-5092-5928-1

A Beluga Stein Mystery, Book Two

Previously Published 2006 by Marietta Press
Published in the United States of America

Dedication

For David Howell.

His sense of humor, quick laugh, intelligence, and his compassion for those who know him is limitless. But it's his keen wit—no matter how many times we share stories of a long-ago bizarre manager who spent each day worried about her 17th century-like towering bleached hair that was stiff enough to cut diamonds—that I'll keep for myself.

Other Books by Wendy W. Webb

Bee Movie
Widow's Walk

Chapter 1

From: Office of Admissions
To: New Students

Dear *Beluga Stein*:
You have been accepted into the Culinary Arts program for the summer term. Attendance at an orientation session is required, so we have taken the liberty of scheduling you for *Tuesday, June 2, 8 a.m. sharp*. If this time is not convenient for you, please notify the admissions office as soon as possible so that an alternate time can be arranged. Space permitting.

Please note, you have been accepted into a specialized program based on the rich heritage of established culinary principles. If you expect to refine your abilities in preparing the typical North Georgia "meat and three," or any variation on cube steak and buttermilk cornbread, you may need to reconsider your acceptance.

We look forward to seeing you on *Tuesday, June 2nd, 8 a.m. sharp*. Really, sharp. Know that your culinary educational experience will be a rewarding one.

Sincerely,
Petula Brock
Admissions

****

The smell could knock you down. Sulfuric odors created such a height and depth that they brought tears to the eyes and choked the smoke alarm. It was as if evil itself entered the room and taken out an eternal lease.

"Save yourself!" yelled Beluga Stein to her feline familiar, Planchette. "Run! Run like the wind and don't look back."

Planchette didn't need to be told twice. Covered in silky black fur that now stood up in points, his sleek body jumped from zero to sixty in a microsecond. Unlike motorized land vehicles, his traction was severely limited by the wet kitchen floor. Four legs moved in warp speed, but the lack of forward motion held him in position like a cartoon still life. Eyes wide, his face was a picture of determination and unadulterated fear.

And then a flailing paw hit a dry patch. He turned into a streak of pure energy, became airborne, and disappeared like a rocket in a Fourth of July fireworks finale.

Hiking up yards of brilliant teal muumuu material to hip level, Beluga tried to follow her cat. Water thrown on the stove to put the fire out now formed an impressive pool on the floor. The trick was determining where the incoming tide stopped and the dry shoreline began. One simple miscalculation and that was it: an investment in orthopedic equipment for a very long time after an equally long hospital stay in a ward filled with hang-gliding, bungee-jumping vacationers. Then, perhaps, she would finally have an answer to who in the world would ever do such things.

Her dream vacation meant cultivating a supine

position wherein one's exertion was limited to raising a hand for another round of umbrella drinks. Life-threatening vacations were better left for others. Others whose thoughts worked in that dimension, or at least in a dimension Beluga preferred to avoid. So, it was a "no" to strenuous activity. Umbrella drinks stayed in the definite "yes" category.

But she'd first have to traverse the many violent eddies created by jagged, peeling pieces of old unnatural flooring before any drinks could be considered.

After one judicious step toward the water, she sighed with deep relief there would be no orthopedic emergency today. Another step, perhaps way too cocky this time, and she sensed the beginning of gravity's relentless and unforgiving pull. No animator need re-create Planchette's cartoon flailing impression since Beluga was doing that all by herself. But being far from the athlete he was, and not nearly as agile, she landed on her backside with a solid *whump* and slid at a great rate of speed toward a nearby wall.

"Stop, stop, stop!"

It was not to be.

The object in motion stayed in motion.

She grazed the table and grabbed a corner of the tablecloth that came away in one motion and billowed like a parachute; took out a chair; upended a display of blooming orchids and one cactus; and slammed into the wall, buffered by a large bag of goat food.

Pausing for a moment to await messages from her neurons that a serious injury had occurred, she got the "all clear" and tentatively tried to hoist herself up. Teal muumuu material stuck to her in wet globs and fought her attempts at standing erect, but she persevered and ultimately won.

The smoke had cleared ever so slightly. But the smell of boiled eggs that had fissured and spewed their burned contents about the stove when the water had long since evaporated had developed a life of its own.

"That's lunch," she announced to the empty room while opening windows with machine gun-like precision. Waving madly as if to usher out the evil smell, she caught sight of the table still pristine and perfectly set for a party of two. "Well, would you look at that? Not a single broken plate. Good to know that if my work as a psychic investigator doesn't pan out, I may have a future in magic."

The front door opened, then slammed shut. Footsteps made by shoes undoubtedly too small and heels dangerously too high tapped across the floor.

"Yoo-hoo. I have arrived. A little late, perhaps, but it was a stunning entrance nonetheless. I just know—"

Words ceased as fast as they had at first been delivered. The sudden silence from a guest would have been embarrassing if it had come from anyone else, but in this case Beluga found it quite agreeable, even as short-lived as it undoubtedly would be.

"Back here, Tanya. Just follow your nose."

Tanya appeared at the edge of the kitchen. Her face puckered as if she had consumed a basket of lemons. Her eyes watered; she dabbed at them with the back of her hand since a talon-length, fire-engine red fingernail used indiscriminately might permanently end her vision. Swaying back and forth on her stiletto heels, she threatened to topple at the slightest breeze.

Finally, after a dry and lengthy swallow, Tanya

regained herself and spoke. "*Poso kani na paro ke ntus?*"

"I can tell you're attempting the language of Greece this time," Beluga said, turning the fan on under the stove hood, "but the message is lost on me. Or should I say, it's Greek to me?"

Tanya sidestepped the pool of water, but overlooked an aberrant splash under one foot that launched her into a high kick that would have made the Rockettes proud. She regained her composure with a tug to her clothes, gulped, brushed her nose a couple of times, and resumed the lemon look. "I said, 'How much does it cost to take a shower?'"

"For friends, nothing. For you I'd have to get a calculator."

"But I see now that a shower is the least of my worries. And since when did you turn your kitchen into a recreational water sport?" Tanya stopped then and turned up her nose. "Calculator, huh? I find that comment vile and insensitive. And, my dearest friend in recent memory, I will add that it was a completely unnecessary crack."

"I could say the same for that cleavage-revealing dress you're wearing. I invited you for lunch, not cocktails at some hedonist's mansion."

"Not that I couldn't fit in at such a place. I have a body to die for much like the other girls."

"Says who?"

"My husbands, for starters."

"But since all six are deceased—"

"Seven. Tragically."

"Since all seven are deceased, well, they aren't talking now, are they?"

"No. They're not talking," Tanya said, with a sly grin. "But know they left this world with smiles on their faces." She winked broadly until one fake eyelash glommed onto her lower lid and effectively glued the eye shut. "*Niotho ponodonto.* I have a toothache."

"Maybe you should reconsider your makeup choices."

"At least I wear makeup now and then rather than your chosen look of death warmed over." She pried her eye open with the edge of a fake fingernail. "It's the smell in here that did it."

"Maybe we should move to another part of the house."

"Don't bother. It's just as bad by the front door as it is in here. What is giving off that noxious smell that eats away eyelash glue?"

"Eggs."

"Next thing you know my skin will slough off."

"Lunch."

"How can you think of food when my attractiveness is at stake?"

"Look at me, Tanya. I always think of food. Soon enough, if all goes well, I'll think of it in terms other than boxes of old, discounted, prepackaged pastries, and cheap luncheon meats. Food groups I treasure, by the way. And since when is your attractiveness not at stake?"

Tanya thought about this a minute to work up an answer. And if Beluga didn't know better, she could have sworn she saw a picture of a light bulb appear over Tanya's head.

"My body is a—"

"Shrine at which you worship. Yeah, yeah. I've

heard that one before."

"You are a despicable woman, Beluga Stein. Positively contemptible and not a little mean." She stuttered for more words, then finally found them. *"Tha sas piraze an kapniza*? Do you mind if I smoke?"

"Not a bit." Beluga lit a cerulean-colored cigarette. "In fact, I'll join you."

"This place smells bad enough as it is without your foul habit."

Beluga inhaled deeply and blew out blue-gray smoke. "I like to think of it as a hobby. Besides it might take the edge off my nerves, and the stench in here."

"A smell you've never explained."

"I told you. Eggs."

"Eggs?"

"They exploded on the stove."

Tanya's eyebrows shot up to her hairline. It was a short trip. "You're not helping your young summer camp students with science experiments again, are you? I thought you learned your lesson with that model volcano and the eerily life-like magma that burned a hole right through your wall."

"I always wanted a bay window."

"In the garage?"

Beluga opened a door to the back porch and waved out more sulfuric fumes. "Just think, if my grad students had free rein with the volcano, this outside area would have been ready to construct a large addition to the house. With a basement. Alas, the eggs weren't an experiment. They were for lunch. But under the circumstances, we'll have to come up with another plan." She spied the large bag of goat food then and went to it. "I wonder…"

"Well, wonder without me. No way will I dine on that. I have a tongue trained to appreciate the fine qualities of imported truffles, and the best *foie gras* money can buy."

"Then your tongue is forked as well. I've seen you eat your weight in sugar wafers and string cheese. And in less than an hour."

"Hear me and hear me well, Beluga Stein. My palate, and other memorable parts of me, will rise in insurrection if you even think about rustling up some goat gruel for me. So put that ugly thought right out of your mind and into Emerson's bowl where it belongs. How is your old goat anyway?"

"One must be creative and open in the culinary arena. He's fine. Hiding out right now, like Planchette."

"Creative and open in the culinary arena certainly describes Emerson. That goat will eat just about anything."

"He once thought Planchette might make a good *hors d'oeuvre*."

"I've seen him look at porch furniture with lust in his eyes, too. That makes him one leaf short of a head of romaine in my book." The thought reached Tanya then. "Wait a minute. What culinary arena?"

"The one in which I'm about to enter."

"What are you talking about?"

"Cooking school. I got the summer off from teaching, so I'm going to see what it's like being a student again."

"You're a professor of biology."

"Now I'll be student of food," Beluga said, scraping off blackened egg from the inside of the pot.

"It'll be hard."

"It'll be fun."

"They might expect you to cook."

"I'm counting on it."

A piece of eggshell lodged under her fingernail. Beluga pried it out with her teeth.

"You can't cook."

"But maybe I can learn."

"You might have to cook eggs."

"Oh." Beluga looked at the mess of yolk and white spattered across the stove and the walls, and the water pooling about her feet. "I didn't think about that."

"Forget cooking school. We can go someplace together this summer. There's a great new health resort and spa I've found in—"

That did it. Beluga had done her time with resorts and was in no hurry to repeat that experience anytime soon. Her mind was made up. Eggs or no eggs, she was going to cooking school.

"I want to do this."

"Or," Tanya said with a taunting wag of a lethal finger, "we can try something different. Like bungee-jumping and hang gliding. It'll take us to heights we've only dreamed of."

"And to falls it'll take the rest of our lives to recover from."

The case of the aberrant vacation thought was solved. The first lemming to the orthopedic ward had been identified. And who else would come up with "heights" as a rationale for certain death or just wishing for death if Beluga had to share a room with her? The thought had come from Tanya, of course, and lodged in Beluga's psyche. But she had no part of it the first time the thought emerged and she wouldn't be swayed now.

"I'm going to cooking school."

"Won't you reconsider?"

"No."

"Pleasepleasepleasepleaseplease."

"No."

Tanya danced in a tight circle while keeping a watchful eye on the water perimeter. "Assisted flight. The wind carrying us like birds."

"And dropping us to the ground to lie dormant and flightless with the rest of the dodos. They're extinct, you know. Undoubtedly the first victims of bungee-jumping and hang gliding."

Tanya stopped her dance and stared. "Are you sure?"

"I can search my biology texts for a reference."

"No. I mean about school."

"I've already been accepted."

"Don't you have to wear a costume?"

"It's not a costume, Tanya. It's a uniform."

Tanya's mouth formed a horrified "o." She pressed her talon-length fingernails over the opening. "Everybody wears the same thing? That can't be. That's not right. It's not natural."

"It's the rule."

"No muumuus then?"

"That is a bit of a problem," Beluga admitted. She hadn't worn anything but muumuus as long as she could remember. In fact, she couldn't come up with even a close approximation of her pants size right now if her life depended on it.

Still, cooking school would be an adventure, and it'd been an awfully long time since she had an adventure that didn't involve finding a dead body. The work of a PI may never be done, but that same Psychic Investigator needed a diversion now and then. Especially when the said PI's moments of insight were, on occasion, elusive.

She was sure of it. Cooking school would be safe from murder.

How could it not be?

And if attendance at school meant taking a muumuu sabbatical while she waded into the murky depths of fitted clothing, well then, that was the price one paid.

Murder-free, safe cooking.

No doubt about it.

Chapter 2

Beluga Stein's Diary

The evil smell lingers.

Even with all the windows in the house open, the doors cracked a notch, the attic fan going full blast, and Planchette's tail fanning his face like he was Egyptian royalty preparing for personal delivery of a peeled grape, the odor of exploded eggs clings to everything like a sock stuck to the back of a shirt by static cling.

Alas, there is no magic laundry cloth to separate one thing from another. So for now I'll have to live with sulfuric fumes and pretend I like them. Or at least pretend they're not there. My choices are severely limited.

Not that I didn't consider Tanya's suggestion to move into a hotel room for the night. I did. Briefly. But my reputation in this small town precedes me, so the various housing entrepreneurs said. In rather unkind tones, I should add.

So what if my reservation for three included a surly goat, a cat with an attitude, and myself? Emerson, while a gifted goat in many ways, has not yet mastered opening a mini bar. Planchette has little interest in watching expensive in-room movies unless there's a female cat in the leading role, and I've been housebroken for months now. So why not take us for the night?

Honestly, people can be so rigid.

Seeing my housing dilemma, Tanya offered myriad excuses rather than the use of one of her many guest rooms. Witness a few of the conversational excerpts: The Blue Room will clash with Emerson's beard. The Pink Room is still not the right shade of pink and so not conducive to a good night's sleep. The Gold Room is far too regal to allow just anyone to stay there.

How about the laundry room? I asked with the barest hint of sarcasm. But she had an excuse for that, too. After the death of one husband in an ugly washing machine incident, she had turned the room into a shrine. To permanently honor him, she had said. And to store winter vegetables.

She's forgotten how long we've known each other. And with that vast amount of time, eons really, comes my personal knowledge that there's only one vegetable that will cross her painted, wrinkled lips: potatoes. The fried variety to boot. I was left with no choice but to tell her, in no uncertain terms, where she could store her winter vegetables.

Best friends: can't live with them, can't live with them.

So, here we are, just the three of us—four if you count the smell. For now all is quiet. Not a creature was stirring. Not even the house. And I with my nightcap had just settled down for a short splintered nap, and suddenly awoke to a pain in my bladder. (Which happens of late when I get nervous, or I have too many nightcaps.)

****

The clatter happened next.

Beluga launched herself out of the tall four-poster at the sound, and effectively missed the step stool that would have eased her safely to the floor. "What? What is it?" She collapsed in a heap on a throw rug, glanced about the dimly lit room in an attempt to isolate the reason for the clatter, then spied it. "Planchette!"

His green eyes glowed from a peep of dawn's first light. Without breaking eye contact, he leaned toward the pile of fallen books and papers and, with measured thought and appropriate follow-up action, proceeded to shred the corner off one particular paper. After chewing with feline contemplation, he finally spat it out and adopted his more natural state of feline contempt.

"Please tell me you haven't consumed an important document."

He blinked once, then continued to stare.

She moved crab-like across the room to the fallen papers, grabbed for it, then squinted to make the words coherent. "Oh. It's just my acceptance letter for cooking school. I was afraid it might be something more important like my grade book, that coupon for coffee, or those negatives of Tanya after the strip tarot card game."

Planchette swatted at the paper in her hands.

"What's gotten into you, boy? Honestly, one could be led to believe something bad was about to happen."

Planchette's eyes narrowed. Then suddenly, without any postural warning of any kind, he let loose a long, ear-splitting yowl that set birds flying from the tree outside the bedroom window.

Emerson was immediately rousted from his sleeping pallet to stand at full red alert. Eyes filled with confusion, he looked from one face to another, then stood at ease by virtue of methodical chewing. He was prepared should any food suddenly materialize, but then he was always prepared for this event.

"Holy crow and cow!" Beluga tapped the date on the paper, then pulled herself up faster than her physique usually allowed. "It's orientation day and there's not a minute to spare if I'm going to be there on time. Move it, Emerson. You'll have to grab a mouthful of breakfast from the new bag in the kitchen on your way out. Make use of your razor claws, Planchette, and open it for him, will you? There's my guys."

Emerson's beard twitched. Planchette swished his tail. They both looked at her as if she'd lost her mind. Right now they weren't far from the truth.

"Late is no way to start a new class. *Move.*"

A scream of claws and hooves on hardwood floors pierced the air. Three bodies of varying sizes tangled, then separated to go different ways, but all moved in a manner most inefficient since organization and time constraints were something they had collectively decided was a lifestyle better suited to others.

"Hurry, hurry, hurry," Beluga told herself, as if announcing the words aloud would make it so.

Pulling a bronze muumuu with an Egyptian motif over her head at the same time she dropped her nightgown to the floor, she figured she'd save herself precious minutes best left for the long drive to the cooking school. She really should have considered springing for a dorm room, but that was then and this was most assuredly a panicked now.

Thank goodness Planchette had kept a watchful eye on the clock. And the date. If left to her own devices she might have showed up hours, if not days, late. And that wouldn't do. Wouldn't do at all.

"Hurry, hurry, hurry."

The uttered words remained useless in turning back the clock, or making time pass slowly, but at least it was something. Now if she could only find those shoes with the Egyptian goddess on the toe…

Perhaps Planchette could be funneled into the business of wake-up calls. Being such a good alarm clock was a gift that shouldn't be wasted. Unless he was sounding an alarm for something else.

Something life-threatening.

"No. Hurry. No. Hurry. No." No, she wouldn't think about that. To think it might allow it to happen.

What could happen?

Nothing. Not a thing. She would just push that growing prickly thought to the back of her mind and focus on getting to the door, then to the car. And if ever there was a day when the 1960s' car, covered in a rainbow of peeling paint colors from countless cosmetic makeovers, needed to cough to life, this was it.

Now if she could only find her pocketbook.

And the car keys.

Chapter 3

Squeezing the multihued car into a spot clearly marked "Faculty," Beluga pulled the emergency brake, yanked the key from the ignition, and waited for the inevitable. There it was. The car gurgled and groaned, then released one last fetid bit of gaseous effluvium before it could rest. Either that or the car had drowned. It was really hard to call.

Reaching for her overnight-sized handbag, she leaned into the driver's side door, popped it open, and waited for the rain of rust to stop lest it fall on her high-top sneakers and settle into her moon and stars socks.

The shoes with the Egyptian goddess on the toes had been the latest casualty of Emerson's voracious appetite. Upon putting him outside for the day, she discovered the mangled shoes draped forlornly across the top of his goat house. Punishment might have been severe and swift by anybody else, but he was a goat, after all, a real cutie, and she was an indulgent mother.

Besides, she never much cared for the shoes to begin with since the goddess figure had a frighteningly similar physiognomy to Tanya. Beluga didn't need to see her friend's mug staring up at her every time a piece of used chewing gum, or worse, had to be coaxed from the tread.

So high-top sneakers it was. And they came in mighty handy now since she had to run to make it up a hill and into the building in time for introductions.

Gasping for breath as if her lungs were about to explode, she found the classroom, wedged herself between the metal chair and its connected half-size writing table, and hoped that this orientation included complimentary lubricant so that she'd be able to get out again. This was clearly not a problem for the skeletal, long-haired young man that sat to her immediate right.

He caught her glance, then offered a handshake and his name. "Tony. My friends call me Tony, for short."

She liked him already. "Beluga Stein. I'm new."

He nodded and waved at the small group. "We all are."

"So you want to be a chef?"

"That's the plan. You?"

"I like to eat," she said, squirming uncomfortably in the tight desk. "A little too much if the fit of this educational torture device is any indication."

"Well, you're in the right place. The school I mean, not the desk."

"I hear the cooks in Scotland can deep fry a mean candy bar. You can't pay enough tuition for that kind of knowledge, I always say."

He locked vivid blue eyes on her. "Do you really always say that?"

"Actually I've never said it before in my life. I guess I'm just a little nervous being a student again. It's been a long time." She studied his youthful looks and the solid black of his long hair that held not a foreshadow of gray. "A really, really long time. What are you? Twelve?"

"I'm twenty. And maybe the student life will come back to you in no time."

"Thank you, Tony. You're very kind and I hope you're right. Although I worry if I can make a cootie catcher anymore."

He gave her a blank, but polite stare.

"Or pass notes in homeroom without getting caught."

The polite stare now held a hint of pity.

"Never mind."

"It'll be okay," he said, graciously dismissing her by opening a notebook and actively seeking a pen that might take hours to find if he had anything to do with it.

Would it be okay? Suddenly she had doubt. Grave doubt.

It was one thing being a student at twenty years of age. It was something far different starting a class at, well, a more advanced and seasoned stage of life.

Having been a professor for so long, she didn't know what being a scholar was like anymore. Perhaps she could study a page from the characteristics of her own students. Sure there was surliness, boredom, an inherent need to leave almost as soon as they arrived, not to mention the various and often creative methods of expressing disapproval when given homework assignments, and the incessant use of like, you know, like using the word "like." But was all this enough of a student model for her to go on now?

More importantly would anyone here be her friend and sit with her at lunch so she didn't have to eat alone? Would she be popular, or a social outcast by virtue of something she could never quite identify?

"Nice outfit."

The voice was female, young of course, like most of the rest of them, and not a little mean in the thinly disguised sarcasm. She took a seat in front of Beluga, then said loudly, "Is that dress a tent maker's reject, or did your mommy make it?"

At least the question of class position was solved. And even the reason this time. Outcast it was. Again. But unlike those dark days of middle school when the mold was set for the rest of her public education, Beluga chose the high road this time.

"No, dear," she said. "None of those. But how kind of you to ask."

The girl snorted, rolled her eyes, and pushed a horseshoe-shaped pierced accessory back into her nostrils.

Tony emerged from his unsuccessful pen hunt to leap into the fray. "Get a life, jackleg."

Beluga's eyes widened. The bully's name was Jackleg? And why, pray tell, would anyone want a horseshoe in their nose?

"Drop dead and die," said the girl.

Ah, that was it. A horseshoe for a horse's ass. High road, Beluga reminded herself while biting her tongue. Take the high road.

Tony looked at Beluga and shrugged. "Sorry. I tried."

"Yes you did, my knight in shining armor."

He offered a slight smile, but the blank look had returned to his eyes.

"You know. The honorable knight arrives to save—"

She stopped her mini lecture before she found herself digressing into the merits and pitfalls of cootie catchers and homeroom note passing. Kids today were so, well, young. Children really. They were just children.

Still, this class would be nothing if not interesting because of the mix of people. But if Jackleg was enrolled in a different class than Beluga, that would be okay, too. Pushed too far, Beluga couldn't be sure there wasn't a side street or two off the high road she might rather take.

But now wasn't the time for revenge thinking. Now was the time to focus on the man standing at the front of the room. He had appeared almost soundlessly from a side door, and instantly commanded such presence that everyone sat a little taller in their plier-like desks.

It was hard to say if this man's presence was the result of confidence, which he exuded from every one of his many pores; girth, which made his entrance from the side door a challenge clearly overcome from previous orientation sessions; or from a colossal ego, which filled the remaining space not taken up by his impressive size. Ned Niblett, British ex-pat, world-renowned chef—so the school catalog said—and director of the culinary program, was a big man. Next to him Beluga could pass for petite and waif-like.

Here, at last, was a kindred spirit in food and stature. Could the recipe for deep fried candy bars be far behind?

It could, and it was.

Ned Niblett stroked his chin, smoothed the crisp white chef's jacket that clung to his body like a second skin, and slid a pair of severe glasses onto his nose for an equally severe and methodical look at those in attendance. He paused on one face, moved to the next, then the next, and seemed gratified to see each victim sink a little lower in their seats at the scrutiny. Finally, as if saving the best for last, he settled on Beluga with a barely perceptible rise of an eyebrow. A minute passed, two, in weighty silence until it was broken when he cleared his throat to announce to those assembled: "I am a professional."

Jackleg muttered under her breath. "That is one scary professional."

He pointed a Ghost of Christmas Future finger at her. "You!" he boomed. "Stand up."

She did. But not without a great deal of support from the back of the metal chair and a trembling hand firmly clenched on the edge of the half-desk.

"What's your name?"

She swallowed dryly, then warbled, "Jeannette?"

"Full name. And be quite sure about it."

"Jeannette Regina Mason." Then as an afterthought, she added: "Sir."

"Why are you here?"

"I, uh—"

"'Uh' is not an answer."

"Because, I...I...well, you see I..." She stood there like an opossum caught in headlights. Speechless, and void of all earlier displays of bravado, if societal pressures were fair and just at all, Jeannette, aka Jackleg, had now been thrust into the role of class pariah.

"*Sit down.*"

She sat swiftly, willingly, and with a tale-tell sign of a perspiration line appearing down the back of her shirt. Beluga almost felt sorry for her.

Ned Niblett's eyes glittered as he surveyed the room for other signs of insurrection. Finding none, he cleared his throat again, then continued. "Has anyone else something to say?"

A sea of heads responded "No way."

"Now then, as I was saying, I am a professional. A professional *cook*. 'Chef' is something to which I still aspire. And, one presumes, something to which each of you aspire or you wouldn't be here. Bloody few will be successful." He paused then as if waiting for some sign of recognition at the gravity of these statements.

A smattering of applause started with Tony, grew to a full pitch as others joined, and ended with a standing ovation sans Beluga.

It wasn't that she didn't appreciate Ned Niblett's appearance today and his honored position within the school, if not the international culinary community. It was more the result of a chair that had, in just these past few moments it seemed, shrunk in size and captured rather sensitive anatomical parts, making expeditious movement an impossibility. A quick escape surely meant pain of the exquisite and lasting type. And a response memorable enough to warrant at least a local headline.

If truth be told, culinary master or not, she didn't know what part of his speech could possibly be standing ovation material anyway. She could find more entertainment and information in a jumping frog competition. Without the frogs.

But now they were all looking at her—staring really—as if wondering what kind of lunatic she was to blatantly disregard such a world class figure as Ned Niblett.

All of them. Staring. Except for the one laughing.

Miss Jackleg herself.

And if Beluga had almost felt sorry for her a while

ago, that feeling was gone now. Jackleg's faux pas was already forgotten, permanently erased in the heat of this bigger debacle.

Beluga Stein, by a unanimous vote, was forever the new class social outcast.

Chapter 4

The paperwork was complete. Everyone had one new picture ID to Beluga's three since she insisted the photographer needed more practice to produce pictures that wouldn't make the "Ten Most Wanted" list. And Ned Niblett had vanished deep into the faculty office catacombs until the next orientation session.

Or, from the size of his ego. A news crew was heard to be on campus.

Beluga realized being the new pariah did have its perks. While most everyone steered clear of personal interaction with her, they also assumed she wouldn't eavesdrop on their conversations. Or that she was as deaf as she was stupid for not standing during an ovation. They were wrong on all accounts.

As a result of their lapse, she found out all kinds of things. Among which was that Jackleg had come here from a brief stint in the CIA. But before Beluga had a chance to inquire about trench coats with epaulets, or agents talking into their wrist microphones while cocking their heads for a reply in the ear piece, she found out the CIA referred to was the Culinary Institute of America. While some of the school's recipes might be secret, the nature of their work was far from covert. So Beluga was relieved she hadn't made a further fool of herself by a misplaced inquiry, but also a little disappointed spies wouldn't be lurking in the hallways.

And she was more than a little curious why Jackleg had left the CIA in the first place.

Holding her oversized handbag to her chest, Beluga sidled up to Tony. "I have a million questions—"

"That many?" he said, walking toward the dining room where the group assembled for a kitchen tour.

"At least. And since you're the only one who'll give me the time of day, I thought I'd ask you."

He looked at his watch. "Eight forty-five."

"No. No, I meant…" She gasped. "Are you kidding me? That's really the time?"

"Waterproof, shockproof, and it just keeps ticking away," he said tapping the watch.

She glanced out the window and covered her eyes as if seeing sunlight would burn a hole through her head. "Morning is a fine time, I guess. It's just that it comes far too early for me. Frankly I'd hoped it was much later than that. Much later."

"We're just getting started."

"I was afraid of that."

He smiled. "What do you want to know?"

"You're not afraid you'll catch cooties by talking to me?" She winked, caught his new absent stare, then scowled. "You know, cooties. A stupid childhood thing akin to plague, if the popular crowd had anything to do with it. Weren't you ever a kid?"

"I don't remember. You had questions? But make it quick, the tour is about to begin."

"Ned Niblett."

"The toughest question first, huh?"

"There's something about him I can't quite put my finger on."

"You and everyone else," Tony said. "But I'll tell you what I know. He's been certified in just about everything in this business. Cooking, pastry, educator, food and beverage, you name it. He's even a Certified Master Chef. There are under a hundred with that title in the entire U.S."

"That all sounds pretty impressive."

"And he's really into fine wines. *Really* into them, but he's an expert in all kinds of spirits."

Beluga nodded. "Now *that* I understand."

"You're an expert in spirits, too?"

"In a manner of speaking." She debated about revealing her part-time role as a psychic investigator, then decided against it. "I daresay I take a vastly different approach to spirits than the one Ned Niblett does, however." She smoothed the growing bulge in her large handbag, whispered into the opening, then continued her conversation with Tony. "How do you know so much about him?"

"He doesn't remember, but I worked in his restaurant one summer a few years ago. He was incredible. A real genius."

"That's why you started that fateful applause and ovation during orientation? Fateful for me, I mean."

"Yeah. In honor of his career, and everything he's accomplished. But things changed at the restaurant. The food critics still loved him, but the staff was a different story. They didn't care he was certified. As far as they were concerned he was certifiable."

"Certifiable? How perfectly fascinating. Some of my best friends are certifiable. Why Ned Niblett?"

"People. People. Gather 'round." A woman wearing a skyscraper-tall white hat over gray-streaked dark brown hair fighting to escape a bun at her neck, waved her arms for everyone to approach. "Over here, please."

"If you don't mind, I'd like to continue this conversation later," Beluga said, but Tony had moved to the head of the amoeba-like crowd for the anticipated tour of the kitchen.

Heading this mission was Chef Pernod. "I am one of few women who have spent a lifetime in professional kitchens all over the world, and I have the credentials to prove it." She cleared her throat and looked around to make sure she had their rapt attention. "My name is Anise Pernod. You may call me Chef Pernod. I am efficient, enthusiastic, and a rule follower. I expect nothing less from my students and, in fact, demand much more."

Like a game show hostess revealing a hidden vowel, she waved expansively across the front of her pristine jacket, taut neckerchief, sharply creased black pants, and ended by pointing at her spit-shined black shoes. "Today will be the last day you'll enter the kitchen without proper attire. This includes the toque— the very symbol of culinary arts. Of course your," she grimaced as if the next word she was about to say would leave a bad aftertaste in her mouth, "*hat* will be significantly shorter than mine, but we'll get to the reasons behind that shortly. If you'll follow me, we shall begin."

Much like following a European tour guide, but without a garish umbrella to keep her wards from going astray, Chef Pernod led the group through one of two swinging doors. "Always, always, go in this door, and out that door. *Always.*"

A female voice piped up from the crowd. "Because you could get knocked out by using the wrong door."

"Some have," Chef Pernod said casually. "Here is the beverage section. Notice the ice machine. Always, always use the plastic scoop. Nothing else. And I mean nothing."

The same voice piped up. "A glass could shatter and you might accidentally swallow a piece."

"Some have," said Chef Pernod.

Beluga eyed the ice machine suspiciously and made a personal note to drink everything at room temperature from now on.

"And this," the chef said upon arriving at a new area, "is the ware washing area. Notice the triple sinks for large items. Over here is the machine that washes plates, utensils, glasses and the like. Clean dishes will come out here at 180 degrees or someone will answer to me."

The commentator spoke again. "You could burn yourself if you're not careful."

"Some have. Scrape leftover food into the large garbage cans. Smaller particles will be consumed by the food disposer here."

She flipped a switch. A jet stream of water spiraled into the sink with a nerve-grinding noise that lasted, by Beluga's calculations, an hour or so. Objectively she knew it would only take minutes to render food back into a molecular state.

Beluga turned expectantly to the commentator and was not disappointed.

"You could lose a finger if you reach down in there." Affixed to her tight sweater was a new photo badge which identified her as Katie Cliff.

Katie, Beluga noted, was young of course, extremely attractive, and clearly had a need to please that was perfectly matched to her thinly disguised competitive nature. She had gotten far in life by virtue of her looks, Beluga sensed, but Katie's compulsion to win at whatever cost would merit a watchful eye.

"Or you could lose an entire hand," Katie added, trolling for praise.

"Some have," agreed Chef Pernod. "Fingers, hands. You name it." A small smile flickered across her lips, then vanished back to a steady state of rarely used facial muscles.

Beluga shuddered. This place was a deathtrap. One misstep and the joy of cooking suddenly became a pain-enhancing, body-threatening, life-altering, multi-organ trauma threat waiting to happen. It was a wonder anyone entered this field without worrying they'd come out on the other side half the person they used to be and on a diet consisting of nothing but liquids sucked up through a straw held by someone else.

"But there's more," the chef said. "Follow me, please."

There was more? What possible horrors were left?

Many, many more, Beluga discovered.

Large gas ovens stood steely vigil under vented hoods while multi-eyed stoves stared without blinking. Devices like "flat tops," and "salamanders," flaunted their seemingly innocent names, but Beluga knew better than to ignore the menace hidden within. Scattered about the kitchen were other treacherous utensils, equipment, and supplies used to create memorable culinary moments since, she hoped anyway, their previous use to extract confessions from hapless victims was no longer needed.

Chef Pernod turned to the gathering with a hint of disappointment that the more impressive part of the tour had come to a close. The only things left to visit were the dry goods pantry and the refrigerators.

The entire group filled the walk-in refrigerator and eyed the shelves filled with dairy products, vegetables, nuts, and defrosting meats.

"Remember, people, and remember this well, a place for everything and everything in its place. And it's always on a shelf. Nothing on the floor. Not one thing, or you'll answer to me. The rules of sanitation procedures are paramount here. Clear?"

A sea of nodding heads indicated they understood.

"Good. I'll hold each and every one of you to it. Last, but not least is the walk-in freezer. You may have a look now."

As she had done at every other station, Katie scooted through the group to arrive at the head of the line first. She pulled the handle on the massive steel door once, to no effect, then popped it open using the weight of her whole body as leverage. A massive cloud of fog billowed into the kitchen like a ghost finally receiving its earned freedom. She gasped at the cloud of cold air that enveloped her and stepped back.

"It tickled me. Something tickled me."

Waving away the thick mist, only now barely clearing, Beluga walked to the freezer when the bulge in her massive handbag started fidgeting, then wildly squirming. "Not now, Planchette."

A scorching yowl came from the bag, followed by the emergence of a round head and pyramidal ears tucked back in alarm.

"What is it, boy? Uh-oh. It's something bad, isn't it?"

He didn't stop to answer, but wriggled free of the bag, jumped to the floor, and tore through the tangle of student legs gathering around to see what all the commotion was about. In seconds he was gone.

"Wait for me in the dining room," Beluga shouted.

Chef Pernod's mouth dropped open. She regained herself quickly, but if she had anything to say about a cat in the kitchen Beluga never heard it.

Katie's voice turned high-pitched. "Isn't anyone listening to me? It tickled me. Something in that... that... freezer came out and touched me."

Beluga stepped into the freezer and felt her breath catch in her lungs. It was cold in here, bitterly cold, but her caught breath was for another reason. She squinted as if her eyes had deceived her, bent over for a better view, and knew what she saw was dead right the first time.

While the shelves contained boxes of meats, fish, and fowl, something far more foul had occurred here. And rather recently by the looks of him. The proof was wedged between the bottom shelf and the floor, and pushed hard against the wall. His skyscraper tall white toque remained firmly in place.

Beluga backed out of the freezer and turned to the group. "Someone should call the police."

Chef Pernod stared at Beluga, then went in to take a look for herself.

Katie said with a lack of enthusiasm, but an unwavering need to be the star of the class, "You could freeze to death in there."

"Some have," Beluga said. "Some have."

Chapter 5

To: Food-Co
From: Culinary Program
Re: Weekly Purchase Order

—Wheat flour, 100 lbs.
—All purpose flour, 100 lbs.
—Sugar, 50 lbs.
—Butter, 50 lbs.
—Eggs, 4 cases
—Body bag, 1

****

Beluga Stein's Diary

Such a day.

And while Chef Pernod tried mightily to restore order with an impromptu lecture on the differences between Grande, Classic and Nouvelle cuisines, I'm afraid the distinctions were lost when the frozen body was wheeled past us to the waiting ambulance.

The sight of such a spectacle took a toll on the chef as well, I should add. Fortunately for me there was no mention of Planchette in the kitchen, but for the rest of us the chef's well-practiced lecture took a sudden nosedive into a stream-of-consciousness series of French words. I think I heard her say that a traditional kitchen brigade had positions with names sounding something like "poisoner," which is rather ominous if you ask me, and "chefs who party," which might warrant further investigation if things start to get dull. Or one finds herself in immediate need of hors d'oeuvres and a tropical cocktail.

Speaking of investigation, there will be one, of course. And I'm guessing it will be far from dull. It seems our John Doe was indeed a John Doe. Or Chef Doe as he's known at the school when speaking in a formal manner. To most of his students he was simply known as "Jack."

Jack Doe always taught the Principles of Cooking class—the one I was forced, rather registered, to take when really Cakes, Pastries and Desserts had my name written all over it. I mean, who wouldn't want to jump right in among all those sweets?

But I digress.

More interesting than the fact he had a deep personal interest in herbs and spices, the more exotic the better, is that the students loved Jack Doe. Really loved him. Downright adored him. All, unfortunately, except for the one among us who doesn't share that sentiment.

It has to be someone among us. Who else would have access to the kitchen but students, faculty, or staff? Unless it's the virtual parade of visitors from the community taking tours of the facility and sampling the wares.

Oh, my. I guess this case might not be as straight forward as I'd hoped. And it is a case. But not one for me.

No way. Probably not. Hopefully not.

Psychic stirrings aside—even as disturbing as it

was when Katie insisted something in the freezer cloud touched her—I really must concentrate my efforts on, if not learning how to be a great cook, at least appreciating those who are. My collection of canned goods have expiration dates older than my adult daughter, Olivia, and my take on fine dining has yet to transcend a basket of fried food delivered to me in a hurry. So I'm far from being certified in anything except frugality and speed eating. But I'm trying. Really I am.

If only those feelings, and those fleeting images of...something would stop. Something...something...but whatever it is eludes me right now.

****

The front door crashed open, admitting Tanya with an armful of bags.

"Toodle-oo, my little meadow muffins," she sang. "*Tha thelate na mu kanete parea ya ena poto*? Would you like to join me for a drink?"

Beluga launched herself from the writing desk like a startled pop-up toy and dropped Planchette from her lap. He landed with all four feet splayed out in escape mode, saw the cause of the injustice, and hissed at her.

"That's right," Beluga said. "Attack. Attack the intruder. I won't stop you."

"The door was open," Tanya said, a bit defensively.

Planchette backed into the shadow of the desk and awaited further orders. His green eyes glowed and never wavered from his potential target.

"The door was most definitely closed. Don't you ever knock?"

"Of course not. Knocking is for minions and

drones and I am neither."

"I hadn't noticed," Beluga said. "I'm getting new locks first thing tomorrow morning."

"I don't think so."

"And why not?"

"First day of class. Remember?"

"Ah, yes."

"No time to wait on skilled help and their strange sense of time." Tanya adopted a brusque version of a deep voice, pushed out her belly, and crossed her arms to imitate contractors she found particularly disagreeable. "Will that be six hours in the morning or six hours in the afternoon that you'll have to wait for me when I have no intention of showing up anyway."

"Yes. I'm afraid our part of the woods is not known for prompt or reliable service."

"Tell me a place that is. And then when he gets here, if he gets here, you'll be an audience of one for this special treat." She pulled her dress pants down and bent over. "The male cleavage endurance test."

Beluga smiled. "That's not always a bad thing."

"Yeah." Tanya adjusted her clothing. "If it's one of those Las Vegas male dancers changing the locks. And do alert me immediately should this unlikely event occur."

"Well, as you pointed out, it won't be tomorrow." She sighed deeply and slumped back into the chair. "Consider it on my 'to do' list."

Tanya pulled out assorted bottles of liquor and mixers from the bag, looked Beluga over carefully, then made a choice. "My first thought was a Tequila Sunrise, but I see now a Zombie might be more in keeping with your demeanor."

"Maybe two."

"I'll get some ice."

Tanya swept up the bottles and headed into the kitchen. In seconds cubes rattled free from their trays and clattered into a metal bowl.

She yelled back from the kitchen. "Second thoughts about cooking school already?"

"Let's just say that among the frozen rows of tenderloins and filets was something of which the meat inspectors would not approve."

Cabinet doors opened and slammed shut. Glasses clinked and separated.

"Honestly, Beluga. Don't you have anything better than old jelly containers around here? We are a civilized people and should act accordingly." Tanya appeared in the room holding a chipped champagne flute and a single tumbler with swaying palms painted across the surface. "And what won't the inspectors approve of? Besides these hideous excuses for drinking vessels?"

"A dead body."

The flute fell from Tanya's hand, and shattered, the round base rolled across the floor and came to rest against the wall. The tumbler took a more direct approach in its total destruction.

Her voice took on a shaky edge. "I'll just get those jelly glasses."

Beluga followed her into the kitchen. "It's happening again."

"What, dear?" Tanya said, as if nothing out of the ordinary had been spoken. Ignoring the obvious was a standard Tanya defensive mechanism, but it never lasted very long.

"A body. Those feelings I get sometimes. Pictures in my mind's eye. And none of it makes sense."

Swilling back the contents poured from an indiscriminate bottle, Tanya paused, caught her breath, and turned to her friend. "You're my best friend in the world, so I trust you to tell me the truth. Is it just you, or does everyone get up in the morning and find themselves in the middle of a murder case?"

"A lot of us did today."

"Swell."

"It's a strange situation, Tanya."

"Aren't they all?"

"Sometimes."

Tanya eyed her.

"Usually."

The look turned to a glare.

"Okay, all the time."

"Spirits?" Tanya handed Beluga a glass.

"Thanks. I think I will."

"No, no. I mean, are there ghosts this time?"

"I'm not getting that feeling."

"But you're getting feelings?"

"A few," Beluga admitted. "But I can't quite put my finger on it."

Wait a minute, where had she said that before? She stopped with the thought. Recently. She had said it recently.

"I'm really not in the mood for another ghost."

"Is there any time you're in the mood for a ghost?"

"No," Tanya said, knocking back her drink. "Can't say that there is. But I'm really not in the mood right now."

"How so?" Beluga eyed Tanya. "There's

something you're not telling me. Spill it."

"All right, all right. Honestly, have you got a bare bulb around here you can shine on me to force a confession?"

"Actually I have quite a few."

"Emerson?" Tanya asked.

"He has a thing for lampshades. Go figure. But you're avoiding the topic at hand. What's going on?"

Tanya sat at the table, twirled the empty jelly glass in her hands. "I'm really thirsty. Can I have another drink?"

Beluga slowly circled the table, then leaned in to her friend using her best TV bad cop impersonation. "You can have all the drinks you want, sister. After. Just tell me the truth. Get it off your chest." She caught the reluctance in Tanya's eyes and decided to escalate the interrogation by slamming her hand on the table. "*Now!* These may be the best days of my life and I will not waste another minute on the likes of you."

Salt and pepper containers shaped like aquatic animals shimmied and jumped.

"When did you get those?" Tanya asked. "I don't remember seeing those before."

"A gift from one of my marine biology students."

"You hurt your hand."

"Not bad," Beluga said. "I was caught up in the heat of the moment, that's all."

"Watching old detective movies again?"

"One or two." She rubbed her hand and offered Tanya a drink. "Look. You have something to tell me or not. It's your call."

"Okay. It's this simple. I figured if you wouldn't take a vacation with me, then I'd take one with you."

"Yes."

"So I signed up at cooking school, too."

"You didn't."

"I did."

Beluga softened immediately. "What a lovely gesture. And incredibly touching. But the answer is no."

"I'll say. I don't want to be a party to a murder case, ghosts or not." She sipped her drink with deep contemplation, then suddenly looked up. "Hey, what do you mean 'no'? I'll go if I want to."

"Tanya, dear heart, your idea of cooking is opening a take-out box. Or ordering something that's not on the menu."

"I have as much skill in the kitchen as you do."

Beluga couldn't argue with that, but she also couldn't argue that Tanya's assistance in murder investigations consisted of brute force and awkwardness—two traits not commonly favored during investigations. Thus she became more liability than asset when it came to P.I. work. And one way or the other, Beluga was sure there would be some type of psychic investigation needed. Somewhere. At some point.

Maybe.

There was little if anything Tanya could offer, and calling it a vacation didn't make it so. The answer would have to stay no.

"I've even rented a little *domatio*, room, for us to stay in. No more commute."

Then again maybe Tanya could offer something.

Certainly on her professorial salary Beluga could never afford elective housing. But there was still one little matter to settle.

"What about Planchette? I never go anywhere without him. And Emerson? What would I do with him?"

Tanya raised her glass. "Taken care of. I arranged for a goat sitter, and Planchette has a new bed. On me. The store only had one left. It's for a small dog and has a bone design—"

A feline yowl sounded from the depths of the living room.

Tanya yelled back. "He'll have to live with it, or fend for himself."

"What classes are you taking?"

"Like you, just one. I told them to surprise me."

"You'll be right in the middle of an investigation."

"Yeah, that's the downside," Tanya admitted. "But think of the adventure. The stories we can tell."

"And if there's a ghost?"

"More stories," Tanya said, with a forced cavalier manner.

"Or if you can't take the heat, as it were, you move out and go home."

"Fair enough. So I'm in?"

"You're in."

Beluga wondered what still lingered that she couldn't put her finger on, but figured she would know soon enough. Perhaps too soon. She clinked glasses with Tanya, and offered a toast.

"Here's hoping neither one of us is in too deep."

Chapter 6

The line formed at the double doors to the kitchen. Beluga took up the rear and couldn't be sure why there was a line, but there was no mistaking the stricken look of each student as they neared the kitchen.

Hitching up the overly large herringbone-patterned chef pants under the too-small, blinding white jacket, she was a picture of worry and supreme discomfort. Where the jacket caught and held any attempt at breath, the pants held a tenuous grasp around her usually ample hips. At any moment the trousers could fall and reveal more than anyone had a right to see.

Such was this fresh hell of wearing supposedly fitted clothes when her last known information regarding specific sizes was ancient history. Muumuus were so much easier, so much more freeing, far more colorful, and they were the one true case where size didn't matter.

The line moved. She stepped forward, hitched up the pants, sucked in minimal breath and released it with a sound akin to a rusty hinge.

A brief pause. Another stricken look as a student passed the double doors. Another step.

Hitch. Suck. Hinge.

Along and along it went until Beluga reached the doors and discovered the source of student discomfort for herself.

Ned Niblett.

Standing like a guard at the gates to the underworld, he scrutinized every student's attire, commented succinctly and to the point, and even sent a few packing to come back when they were suitably suited up.

"Name?" he asked, as Beluga approached.

"Stein. Beluga Stein."

He scanned the list attached to a clipboard, made a notation, then started an unblinking examination of her. "Redo the neckerchief. Too sloppy. Jacket clean, but a bit of a tight fit wouldn't you say?"

"What space I lack in the jacket is more than made up for in the pants."

He eyed her carefully. "Indeed." His pen was poised ready for another notation when suddenly it escaped his grasp and landed some feet behind him. "Bloody hell."

Beluga stared wide-eyed. If she hadn't seen it for herself, she would have never believed it possible. The chef had no more thrown the pen than she had. It had simply freed itself, become airborne, and landed in a perfect line behind him. More astonishing was the fact that Ned Niblett seemed minimally concerned, as if this was far from a rare occurrence.

Students frantically scrambled to retrieve the pen and return it to its rightful owner, but only one was quick enough.

"Here you are, sir," Katie Cliff said, handing him the pen. The smile on her face clearly indicated she expected praise for a job well done.

Ned Niblett would not deliver. Pushing his glasses further up his nose, he turned to the girl and bellowed,

"*Mise en place*. You should be working on your *mise* instead of standing about like a lackey. Get to it. Now."

Katie Cliff nodded ever so slightly and slunk around the corner to the kitchen.

He turned back to Beluga. "Now, then. Name."

"Beluga Stein."

He scanned the list in front of him. "There are two of you then?"

"No," she said. "Just the one. But there's plenty of me to go around."

"Indeed." He marked the list, then cocked his head. "You'll be on the other side of the kitchen. My class. Start your *mise*. The list is on the board."

"Aye, aye, Captain. And what exactly is *mise*? I'm guessing it's not the plural of 'me.'"

"Get to it. *Now*. Next."

Horrors upon horrors. The great and powerful Ned Niblett was teaching her class. She knew things were in an uproar after the untimely demise of Jack Doe, but the head of the program was teaching a class? This had to be unheard of. Beluga didn't wait long to find out how right she was.

Tony barreled around the corner with a large stainless steel pan bearing a pile of vegetables. "Chef Niblett is teaching the principles of cooking class. It's unheard of."

"You read my mind." Beluga scrambled after Tony like a ravenous tourist at an all-you-can-eat buffet that was about to shut down for the night. "One hopes his teaching is a temporary situation."

Tony smiled. "I hope it isn't. There's a lot we can learn from him."

"Like arrogance?"

"It goes with the chef territory."

Beluga had broken into a run to keep up with the young man as he went from the refrigerator to a large stainless steel table and back. She stopped, grabbed him by the arm—hitch, suck, hinge—and demanded an answer. "Why, pray tell, are we attempting to mimic an Olympic sprinter?"

"The *mise*."

This time it was Beluga's turn to render a blank, but polite stare.

"That's short for *mise en place*. Technically it means 'everything in its place,' but in reality it means getting your shit together so you can start cooking."

"Funny how I understand each individual word you spoke, yet the greater concept has escaped me."

"It gets worse. You have to do it fast. Everything in the kitchen is fast." Tony reached for a large knife out of a kit, started cutting up vegetables at a rapid and well-practiced clip, then cocked his head toward a blackboard at the front of the kitchen. "There's the list."

Beluga scanned the board. "Two pounds onions. One pound each of carrots and celery. Large dice." She looked at the growing pile of cut vegetables accumulating in front of Tony. "Well, it looks like you've taken care of the produce just fine. Now if you'll tell me where I can find a pair of large dice, and why playing craps is part of cooking school, I'll just finish up this little assignment."

The pity returned to Tony's eyes. "Large dice is the way the vegetables have to be cut up. And that amount is per student."

"Great Ganesha! You've got to be kidding me."

"We're making *mire poix*."

45

"And that would be…?"

"Flavoring for the stocks. Which can then be made into sauces." He scooped the diced vegetables into a larger pan. "You really don't have a clue, do you?"

"In more ways than one, my friend. Anything else I should know?"

"Cats aren't allowed in the kitchen."

"I guessed as much. But it beats me why that should be since Planchette is meticulous in his grooming, and more hygienically sound than most people I know. But not to worry. My feline familiar is taking the day off. Resting, one hopes, on his dog bed. Which he hates. Not the resting part. He hates the dog bed."

"Um hmm," Tony said distractedly.

"The dog bed was a gift from Tanya. I didn't want to hurt her feelings, but the truth is Planchette prefers to sleep on a Ouija board. And sometimes he actually uses it to make predictions, which is no small feat since he doesn't read, but there you are."

"There you are," Tony said, so absorbed in his work that he appeared not to comprehend anything she said.

"I wouldn't be surprised if cats ruled the world one day. Some could argue that not having an opposable thumb makes things more difficult for them, but they'll overcome that one day, I'm sure."

"I'm sure." He looked at the clock on the wall. "There's one more thing. You've got twenty minutes to complete your *mise*. And don't forget your toque. That's your hat."

Beluga gasped and set to work.

Tony had been true to his timing, except that

twenty minutes in this frantic kitchen translated to what seemed like seconds. Before Beluga knew it, Ned Niblett was upon them to review their work.

Going from one station to the next, he eyed the vegetables and the student, and didn't hold back on his many, yet rather unvaried opinions.

"Too big," he said to a beaming Katie Cliff. Her smile became instantly frozen on her face.

"Too small," he said to an older man who remained expressionless.

"Too uneven." On and on he went using such declarations as ragged, sloppy, and butchered. He stopped in front of Tony, looked over the vegetables and announced with faint praise: "Hmm. Not bad."

Tony nodded ever so perceptibly.

But then it was Beluga's turn.

"I'll have a look now," he said, "if you'll kindly remove your upper body from covering the table."

"I'd rather not," she said.

"But I insist."

"I'm new."

"And I'm quite aware of that fact."

"Are you?" she asked. "Because it seems to me your expectations are a tad higher than my current capabilities."

"I'm a professional."

"So you've said."

"I'll have that look now."

Hitch, suck, hinge. Beluga rose slowly from the table while her toque slowly slid down her face to rest on the top of her ears and across the bridge of her nose. The visual disturbance was for the best, she decided. She didn't want to see the expression on Ned Niblett's face anyway. The carrots, celery and onions, as required, were all there, they just remained in a natural state, save for the two onions she had managed to destroy while attempting to peel them.

A snicker came from between equipment that separated the two sides of the kitchen.

Beluga pushed up her toque in time to see the leering face of her new nemesis, Jackleg. But now she could see Ned Niblett as well. His expression was far from leering. If anything it held confusion, a little bit of worry, and a great deal of annoyance. And then Beluga saw why.

The massacred onions rocked back and forth as if gaining momentum for an act that was most unvegetable-like. Then, sure enough it happened. One onion rolled across the table at bowling speed and took out a pile of another student's vegetable dice in a perfect strike. The other onion stopped moving suddenly, as if an unseen hand held it firmly in place.

All eyes, including those of Jackleg and Ned Niblett, stared at the onion and waited.

A second passed. A minute.

Breath held was collectively released, and a few students began to tentatively return to their work.

Beluga couldn't be sure since the vision was so fleeting, but if pressed, she might say there *was* a hand on that onion. A small hand, strong. Masculine perhaps. And maybe, just maybe, that hand was raising the mangled onion from the table to—

A rap sounded on the glass that allowed visitors a view of the kitchen from the dining room.

All heads turned to see the source of the disruption.

Tanya waved, voiced a silent "yoo-hoo," but the

look on her face was far from pleased.

The onion sallied through the air and landed on the glass with a wet splash. If Tanya's face had a bullseye drawn on it the landing couldn't have been more exact. As it was, she stepped back, saw the smear of onion juice running down the glass, and appeared to draw herself up for what would surely be a temper tantrum of epic proportions.

A light as air giggle came from…where?

Beluga looked around, but couldn't isolate the sound. Or the source. The hair on her neck and forearms stood at attention.

Another giggle.

"Blast," Ned Niblett said. "It's back."

Katie Cliff's words were at once labored and whiny. "Did it touch anyone? Please say no."

Then, like a tornado, unexpected and destructive, a curved path that danced this way and that appeared in the wake of flying vegetables and overturned stainless steel pans. Small dice, large dice, ragged, sloppy or butchered, it didn't matter. Organic matter was propelled over tables, sailed across the floor, and even spattered over what moments ago were blinding white, pristine chef jackets.

And then it stopped.

It was here, Beluga discovered, that Ned Niblett was equally adept at stopping a surprised reaction in favor of starting a full authoritarian recovery.

"Clean this up now," he yelled. "Start the stocks." He watched briefly to see his orders initiated, then took his leave just as Tanya entered.

"How dare you," she said.

"Not now, Tanya."

Her lips curled back into a snarl. "How dare you embarrass me like that."

Beluga grabbed a towel and started cleaning the glass. "I had nothing to do with it."

"Didn't you?" Her voice rose an octave. "Didn't you?"

"If you screech any higher, dogs from two counties over will start to show up."

Tanya's lips moved, formed words, but no sound was forthcoming.

"I can hear their thundering paws now. Running. Coming to see who's calling."

Jackleg snickered from between the kitchen equipment.

Tanya turned on her. "You want a piece of me?"

The girl's eyes widened.

"Come over here, you little snot. I'll show you what's what. Or don't you have anything better to do?"

Jackleg shrugged nervously. "Bread class. I'm waiting for my rolls to rise."

"Well, do it somewhere else."

"I can't."

Tanya waggled her fingers at the girl. "See these?" The waggling picked up speed. "Itchy fingers. And they're telling me they want a piece of you if I see you again. Got it?"

The girl nodded her head like a dashboard dog. The horseshoe nose ring dropped out from inside her nostrils. She pushed it back, then hastened to return to her side of the kitchen.

"Well done, Tanya. Who knew that the way to deal with a bully is to bully them right back."

"Remind me to pass on the bread when lunch is

served."

"Better now?" Beluga said, turning her attention to the mess on the table. "The tantrum passed?"

"Give me an onion to throw at you and I'll let you know."

"I didn't throw it."

"I saw you."

"You saw it come from my direction, but trust me, my hand was not behind the pitch."

"Whose hand was it, then?"

Beluga shrugged. "Well, that's kinda the problem."

"You know what? Never mind. I don't want to know." She scanned the frantic activity in the kitchen, and the mess they were attempting to clean. "What in the world happened here?"

"You might say that's the rest of the problem."

Tanya whistled. "And I thought food fights only happened at summer camp."

"Yeah. But the ammunition here is better. And it has fancier names."

"There's no one who'll own up to the cause?"

"Not yet."

"I'm guessing you have a theory. And I'm guessing there's a supernatural basis to that theory."

"Too early to say."

"Too early to say because you don't know for sure, or you don't want to say it aloud knowing that I'm weak, vulnerable, in immediate need of a stiff drink, and that such information could put me over the brink?"

"Yes."

"We're going around in circles, Beluga."

"Yes." She stopped scooping vegetables from the floor and turned to Tanya. "A stiff drink? Now? And why, by the way, aren't you in the kitchen?"

"My surprise class."

"Not cooking?"

"And not eating again after what I just saw."

Beluga hitched her pants, sucked in a breath, and released it with a hinge noise that could only come from the dying breath of a woman wearing an obscenely small chef's jacket. "Now who's talking in a circular manner?"

"Safe eating. Are you happy now?"

"Thrilled. And if I could breathe, maybe get a little air to my brain cells, I might even figure out what you're talking about."

"Aren't you listening to me?"

"Just a minute." Beluga slid open the buttons on her jacket, relaxed her belly, and gulped a deep breath as if she had been a drowning victim popped to the water's surface just before it was too late. "That feels so wonderful."

"You never listen to me."

"I'm all ears now, Tanya."

"Surgery can do wonders," she said dryly. "They signed me up for a safe eating class. It's called Safe Eating. It's a class. We just look at pictures of awful things that grow in food. Or grows in the people that cook the food. Chef Pernod is the teacher and I think she actually loves this stuff. Thrives on it, in fact." Tanya shuddered. "A stiff drink is my only recourse. And if I find out there's something nasty that grows in alcohol, life will simply end. *Pffft*. Just like that."

"It can't be that bad."

"It's worse. Break is almost over and we're going to see a movie next. Can you believe that? Someone actually made a movie about germs? What? They don't have anything better to do with a degree in filmmaking?"

"Maybe they don't. But I do." Beluga reluctantly started the uncomfortable process of buttoning up her jacket. "See you at lunch?"

Tanya waved over her shoulder as she slouched out of the kitchen. "It's what you don't see that should worry you."

What you don't see. Like the cause of flying vegetables? There was a cause, and most definitely an effect. But there was also a growing list of unanswered questions, too, about the reason behind both these things.

She sucked in a breath, held it, then closed the final jacket button on her self-inflicted suffocation.

Suffocation. Respiratory paralysis. Could it be that Jack Doe suffered these things?

The thought was there, clear as... clear as... damn. It was clear as mud. No amount of chasing thoughts around in her mind brought back that moment when she almost had a big picture. But was she right? Or even close? And if he had died from suffocation, or something similar, was it self-induced or was it murder?

More questions. And more questions made it painfully obvious there were plenty of answers yet to be discovered.

There was nothing left now but to start snooping around. To get anywhere meant her investigation would have to be kicked up a notch. And then *bam,* maybe she'd figure out the death in the freezer and the vegetable insurrection in the kitchen.

Maybe.

"Twenty pounds of bones," Tony said in passing.

"Beg your pardon."

"For the stock. Your share is twenty pounds of bones. We've got to get everything going or there's no lunch break."

Lunch. Now that sounded pleasant. At least then she could get off her feet for a few minutes, and if things went well, make inquiries of a few minds. "Your wish is my command."

His back was turned, but Beluga knew there would be pity in his eyes. No matter. What better place to solve a kitchen mystery than in the kitchen. First stop, freezer. For the bones.

And perhaps a clue or two.

Chapter 7

The stocks were simmering and the first wave of bread had been proofed and baked.

Lunch was served.

Such as it was with the time allowed to consume it.

The Principles class had their hands full with the aftermath of the vegetable mêlée and the impending need to prepare assorted bones for the many stocks, so lunch plans were left to the bakers.

While the bakers started their day with an equal frenzy of activity, things suddenly came to an abrupt halt while their products did whatever hoodoo they did that caused them to rise. The frenzy began anew when it came time for baking, then halted just as suddenly when it came time for cooling. So it was that the bakers had the spare time to prepare lunch today.

And they were nothing if not students who knew how to prepare foods that filled up other students. Bakers were a funny breed.

Beluga ransacked a tray of rolls in various shapes. Bread products of all sorts were in their blood, she decided as she piled pasta on her plate, covered it with a white cheese sauce, and noticed there wasn't a green vegetable anywhere to be seen. If the edibles weren't a member of the brown food group, bakers, it seemed, weren't interested.

Beluga couldn't be happier. Her jacket had taken a

mini sabbatical from her grateful body; the food would stop her growling stomach; and taking a seat, however briefly, would be welcome relief to her aching feet. If she never stepped foot in a commercial kitchen again, she would at least be more appreciative of those who did it day after day. And she had a pile of the brown food group on her plate to prove it.

She took a seat at a circular table at one end of the dining room. The other side of the room was reserved for paying patrons when a meal service was offered. The lines, though never spoken aloud, were clearly drawn: us versus them. Cooks at this end of the room versus paying eaters at the other end.

But there was another unspoken line here as well. At least today. No chef instructors joined the lunching students. The baking chef was ushered off to his office for some uncompleted paperwork needing priority attention; Chef Pernod was, perhaps, putting together a musical celebration to bacteria; and Ned Niblett was nowhere to be seen. After his blunt departure from the kitchen earlier that morning, the head chef had yet to return.

Strange.

And stranger still—to Beluga anyway—was the fact she occupied a table all to herself. Other students made a point of squeezing in around already packed tables as if they were carefully avoiding her. And perhaps they were avoiding her. One day of class did not a pariah unmake.

"There's room here," she said, waving at an empty chair to a passing student.

The student shook her head and moved on to a crowded table nearby.

"Plenty of space."

Another student ignored Beluga's invitation completely and found a wobbly chair that seemed to offer more safety then joining her.

"Pull up a seat."

This time he did. It was the one older man in her cooking class.

"I'm Beluga Stein," she said, offering her hand.

"Burton Smith." He accepted the handshake, then focused his attention on his modest helping.

"So where are you from and why are you here?" Beluga asked, grateful for any conversation.

"I don't like to talk much."

Tanya loomed suddenly and directed her lust at the man. "Well, I'll talk for the both of us tall, gray and the silent type."

"Not now, Tanya."

"Why not now?" Tanya slid into the seat next to Burton and leaned close. "She's pushy, but harmless. I, on the other hand, am far from harmless. Tell me you don't love hearing that."

He pushed pasta into his mouth to avoid comment.

"Aren't you going to eat?" Beluga asked.

"Not that stuff. Not on your life," Tanya said. "And not after that film I just saw. Do you have any idea what grows in starchy foods? I do." She touched Burton's arm and whispered. "Let's just say I hope the temperature of your lunch reached the appropriate level or you'll want to pass on dancing for a few days."

He stopped chewing briefly, then swallowed hard.

"Don't you worry," she said, patting him. "You can share my lunch." She reached into her purse and pulled out an impressive array of candy bars from a vending machine. "Chocolate. Chocolate with nougat. Candy-coated chocolate. And my favorite, chocolate with a soft cream center."

He tentatively reached for a candy bar.

She winked at him. "Some think chocolate is an aphrodisiac. What do you say we find out if that's true?"

"Tanya!"

Burton mumbled something under his breath and reached for his plate as he rose to leave.

Tanya pulled him back to his seat. "Tall, gray, silent, and shy. I like that in a man."

He looked at her then. "I'm spoken for."

"Say it isn't true," Tanya said, slumping in her seat as if shot.

"Afraid so."

"A good, solid relationship is nothing to be afraid of," Beluga said. "Just ask Tanya. She's had more than everyone in this room combined."

The man's eyebrows rose. "That so?"

Tanya smiled at him, then glared at Beluga.

"How so?" he asked.

She reached for a candy bar, ripped open the package with her teeth, and took a bite. "How else? Chocolate."

"I don't much care for chocolate."

"Pity."

"It starts out as a yellow pod on the cacao tree, then it's dried and fermented, and then roasted. Did you know that?" he asked.

Tanya's eyes glazed over.

"I personally had no idea, so find that information absolutely delightful. Isn't it, Tanya?"

Tanya stifled a yawn.

"Isn't it, dear?" Beluga said, launching a blow aimed at Tanya's shin.

"Ouch." She snarled at Beluga, "Who knew candy could be such a kick?" then turned her attention back to the man. "So, Burton, how did you come across this fascinating information?"

"Chef Doe."

Beluga stood straight up. Plates and glasses on the table rocked dangerously.

"Chef Doe? Jack Doe? You talked to him?"

Burton seemed nonplussed. "All the time. At least it used to be all the time."

"Recently?"

"Really, Beluga," Tanya said. "You're making a scene. Sit down and calm yourself."

She sat, cleared her throat, and proceeded. "Did you talk to him before, I mean, just before—"

"He was murdered? Hard to say."

"Try, Burton. It'll get easier the more you talk. I promise."

"I saw him the night before."

"And—"

"And we talked. That's all."

"But you don't like to talk."

"Not much."

Beluga rubbed her eyes. "Honestly, Burton, I can pull out my own teeth with tweezers faster than this conversation is moving along."

"Why do you want to know?"

She paused then. Because a soul had been sent adrift before its time? Because every intuitive cell in her body told her it was murder, and that freezer burn is not a natural cause of death? She took a breath and gave it her best shot.

"Because you think it was murder, too."

"I didn't say that," Burton said.

"Oh, but you did."

Tanya piped up then. "I heard you."

Confusion flickered across his face.

"And I agree." Beluga said. "So whatever we can do to find the killer, and make this right, we have to do it."

"We were two men talking. That's all."

"The topics, Burton. What were the topics?"

"House renovation mostly. That's what I do while I get some chef training. I did some work for him. He has an old cabin that needed some work."

"What else?" Tanya asked.

Beluga turned to her. "I can handle this."

Tanya blew a raspberry. "You're handling it so well that we can be here for decades while we explore the joys of bathroom plumbing."

"Oh. And you can do this so much better?"

"Better than you, dear heart. And in at least half the time. Wait. That didn't come out right."

"It rarely does, Tanya."

Burton raised a hand to stop them. "And we talked about women."

"Women?" Tanya and Beluga said together.

"He was having problems with his girlfriend. They were arguing, he said. She's a student here. And that's all I know."

"But—"

"That's all I know." He stood, picked up his plate, and looked at Beluga. "That's all I can do." And then he disappeared into the kitchen.

A student? Chef Doe was having a thing with a student? Was that allowed? That kind of behavior was most distinctly not allowed at the college where she taught. By some of the faculties' more loosely defined interpretation, a thing with a student was at least frowned upon—especially if they got caught. But here, under the circumstances, a whole new wrinkle had developed. Beluga sat still as stone and speechless. Now what?

She didn't have to wait long.

Tanya rose from her seat and tapped a glass with a fork. "May I have your attention, please? Your attention. Thank you."

The students quieted and watched her.

"*Borite na mu sistisete ena kalo bar*? Can you recommend a good bar? No? Well, here's another option you might be interested in. Beluga and I will be hosting a party in our suite tonight, and we'd like to invite all of you to attend. Drinks and food will be provided."

A small cheer went up.

Tanya smiled broadly and bowed. "Thank you for your attention. We'll see you at eight."

The frenetic activity of cleaning and finishing up the cooking for the day was on. But this time a few students had the graciousness to high-five Tanya in passing, and nod curtly at Beluga on their way back to the kitchen.

"What party?" Beluga asked.

"Why the one we're giving tonight, of course."

"Tell me again why we're having a party?"

"To flush out your chef's girlfriend, naturally."

"I see. And we'll hold this party in our suite?"

"Dorm sounded so, well, hollow. Frankly 'jail cell' is more an apt description, but who wants to party in a jail cell?"

"Prisoners?"

"Besides, dear," Tanya said, ignoring her, "we really must do something about your status around here. No one seems to like you."

"You noticed, huh?"

"Each and every time we're together."

"Gee, thanks."

"Not to worry. If they like me, there's a good shot they'll tolerate you. And wouldn't that make things infinitely easier to find the murderer?"

"Possibly."

Tanya picked up her purse. "I'm through for the day, thank goodness, so I'll start searching for a caterer who has seen the germ film and is in need of last minute cash. You'll be sure to clean up those candy wrappers for me, won't you? There's a dear." She turned to leave, then stopped with one last salvo. "What would you do without me?"

"I can't begin to guess, but my imagination is very fertile."

"This case wouldn't be anywhere without me. Toodle-oo."

Brute force and awkwardness. That was Tanya to the "T." But sometimes an investigation called for other things.

Beluga reached into her pocket to touch the plant stem she'd found on the floor of the freezer.

Sometimes an investigation called for an eagle eye and a hunch.

And sometimes it called for an expert who could help. Even if that expert was considered, by all accounts, "not right."

She just hoped he'd be wearing clothes this time.

Chapter 8

The approach to the house wasn't exactly like the one in Daphne du Maurier's description of Manderley, but it was close enough.

And while Beluga didn't dream of this place last night, or any other night, it was hard to forget once you'd been there. That is if you remembered where it was in the first place.

"Damn, damn, damn." She stopped the car on the side of a heavily wooded road, and could imagine multicolored peeling paint disturbing otherwise pristine fauna. She pulled the directions out from under Planchette. "It's got to be around here somewhere. But where exactly? You know, a mile marker wouldn't kill anyone. I'd even be happy to see an animated waving hand pointing to the entrance."

Planchette yowled and stood against the passenger side glass.

"Over there? Are you sure?"

He pawed the glass at a rapid clip with both front feet.

"Okay. Okay. I get it." She nudged the wheezing vehicle into some semblance of forward motion and peered through the woods for the gate. "What do you see in old Doc anyway?"

Planchette looked at her with unblinking green eyes.

"I mean besides the fact you'd trade my lap for his any day."

He winked.

She smiled. "You're a traitor, you know that. Ah, there's the turn off. And the gate."

The car groaned and shimmied as it turned right, and was met by a closed wrought iron fence that was vastly wide as it was tall. Curlicues decorated the fence. If one dared look close enough at the design, one could easily imagine stick figure people engaging in various forms of debauchery.

"Yup. This is the place. And I still maintain that some of those positions are not physically possible." She jabbed at a speaker button, waited, then yelled at the box while waving at a camera tucked among the branches of a large hemlock. "Let me in or I'll tell everyone you cheat at tarot blackjack."

Large hinges screeched as the gate slowly opened.

Coaxing the car to hang in there through the long entrance drive with a promise of a respite at the end, she looked into the rearview mirror and saw the gate close behind her. If she hadn't been here before, granted a long time ago, the entire scenario would give her pause. But as one eccentric to another, this was all in a day's work. Fortunately Doc's unconventional behavior didn't include practicing medicine anymore, so almost everyone was safe now. Instead he focused his attention on exotic plants lovingly cared for in his own personal conservatory.

The road to this turnoff had occurred during a late afternoon with a bright summer sun. The approach to the house was a different matter. What started as stately hemlocks turned into a tangled canopy of old oaks, scruffy pines, unkempt magnolias, rhododendron, and other overgrown underbrush that had become tree-like years ago. The effect was a sudden plummet into darkness. Beluga squinted to regain some form of usable vision to avoid the worst potholes on a once pristine paved driveway. One false move and she'd find herself dropped into a bottomless sea of ivy, never to be found again.

Old Doc loved this entrance just the way it was. Or even better, what it would ultimately become. He insisted the jungle-like atmosphere gave the place character. Beluga knew it was to keep uninvited characters out.

Quite effectively, she realized, as a bird of prey swooped past.

No pizza deliveries came here. Even mail service had long since stopped. In one unfortunate case the arrival of an expensive European antique was left appropriately crated, but forlorn and unsigned for, outside the unusual gate. Had it not been for the arrival of guests to Doc's memorable "Come as You Were" reincarnation party, the packaged French armoire might have become a victim of overzealous plant growth, wildlife with sharp teeth and unrestrained colons, and other hostile environmental influences.

She rounded a small bend in the drive, bumped over a fallen branch, and caught a partial glimpse of the house façade. Gone. There again. Gone again. The place was tantalizingly close, but she had been fooled before. There was still another quarter mile left in this trek, and at the rate she was going and the sad condition of the road, it would be another good ten minutes to get there.

Just once, she wished, just once it would be nice to travel a main thoroughfare and pull up at a friend's simple dwelling without the need for a change of clothes and directional technology. Of course she had such a friend once. Long, long ago. Bitter Root, as he called himself, was the first one by all modern accounts who lived in a pre-fab teepee. Sweat lodges had not yet become a need among weekend visionaries, so instead he found his time spent convincing parents of young children that his modest abode was a personal residence and not an inflatable rest stop/playground trampoline to break up a long drive. Ultimately he moved to an area so remote even he didn't know where it was, and Beluga never saw him again.

Not that she could blame anyone for wanting a little privacy, but enough was enough. For all the foo-rah involved in getting to Doc's place, the truth was he loved city life and all the cultural amenities a city offered. His forays into big populations, both domestic and international, were often. When he wanted personal space, however, he didn't mess around.

Perhaps it was his proclivity toward nudity that prompted this hermit-like choice.

Or his conservatory filled with carnivorous plants and other dangerous, if not downright lethal, flora.

Hard to say really.

Whatever his strange leanings, he was still a wealth of curious information when one was in the market for such. Doc was also a wealth of wealth. Some said his impressive finances were the result of intercontinental clientele wanting unusual and costly treatments, while others claimed he inherited both house and money. At the very least he was a memorable host of extraordinary events for reasons expected, but more often completely irrational. The latter being far more entertaining, of course.

Afternoon tea, an affair she expected to experience today, would be perhaps the most low-keyed interaction she had ever had with Doc. Since she was here on business, a like-minded approach would be the most appropriate. Even if it meant self-restraint on both their parts.

The life of a psychic investigator wasn't all festive hats and party favors. In fact, it was never those things. Well, almost never. Rarely. Sometimes just the thought of frivolity kept a P.I. going during the low points. It was healthy, needed. Otherwise the stress wreaked havoc with intuition and that would never do.

"Right, Planchette?"

He ignored her while keeping his gaze firmly fixed on the house that loomed ahead.

"Looks like we're here."

She opened the door to the car. A rush of fur and sleek musculature over her lap, and a last second swat of his tail against her cheek brought Planchette to the front door before she had a chance to undo her seatbelt or wait for the engine cough to stop. While waiting for the last eructation, she looked up at the sky and noticed the sun again. Funny, but it always seemed to her that no matter the time of day or month, there should be a constant full moon sitting vigil and judgmental over this place.

Ah, well. Judicious reasoning would have to be left to Doc. He knew how to hand it out with the best of them.

The car snorted, then sniffled, and fell quiet. She

gathered her ample handbag and walked to the double front door of the rambling, multi-leveled house, and reached out to pull the cord that was the doorbell. The door swung open and Planchette became instantly airborne.

"There's my fellow," Doc said, catching the cat. "Missed me, did you?"

Planchette rolled over in Doc's arms so that his legs stuck out at relaxed angles and his tail curved like a closed parenthesis. A sappy, satisfied look settled on his feline face similar to the one on Beluga's face. Doc was a handsome man, not a bit hard on the eyes. Except for the occasional feral look that settled in his eyes, and a rather disconcerting and random appearing tic, he was a dead ringer for Sean Connery.

"Yes, I see you have missed me. Ditto. And you're right on time for tea. Yours, Master Planchette," he said, walking through a great foyer and into a sitting room, "will not be the brewed kind, but I trust you'll enjoy it more for just that reason."

Three wingback chairs were congregated around a circular table laden with goodies. Doc gently placed Planchette on a chair and, with great drama, whisked away a silver top to reveal a crystal champagne glass filled with fresh catnip and a side of poached salmon. Planchette sniffed briefly, then started a delicate and mannered chewing.

Doc waved Beluga into a chair and offered her a cup of tea. She accepted with a raised eyebrow.

"I can't help notice that Planchette's service is imported crystal, but mine is most definitely of a domestic quality. Plastic, I believe."

"You always had quite the eye for details, my

dear."

"Any reason for this?"

"One gives as one gets. I am merely trying to assure your comfort in making you feel at home."

"But I don't want to feel like I'm at home right now. I'm here. And I know there's imported, devastatingly expensive china and crystal all over this place."

"I will be partaking from the former. You will stick with cartoon character plastic. There's even a matching plate that I trust you'll use for the sandwiches and pastries. And don't lick your fingers when you're done. It's so... common. Not to mention hygienically unsound."

"Planchette licks the back of his legs."

"It's his nature."

"Your point?"

Doc sipped his tea soundlessly and slid a watercress sandwich onto his plate. "When you've achieved the agility necessary for licking the back of your legs, I will, as it were, reconsider my position."

"You're a snob."

"Siren."

"Pompous ass."

"Harlot."

They stared at each other, then broke into sudden laughter and hugged.

"It's been a long time, Doc."

"Too long."

"How did we let time get away from us like that?"

"I travel. You teach. It happens."

"We really must get together more often."

"I'm thinking of having another party soon."

Beluga snatched a gooey pastry from the silver tier, popped it onto her mouth, brought her fingers to her lips, but stopped before the licking infraction occurred. Instead, she wiped her hand on her muumuu. The papaya pattern against a sunset background would conceal most anything. "Fabulous. What kind of party?"

He dabbed a linen napkin to his mouth and nodded discreetly to indicate an aberrant food item needed her immediate attention.

"Oh. Sorry." She wiped her mouth with the back of her hand.

He licked his lips and pointed at her upper lip.

"Still there?" Her hand took another pass. "Gone now?"

Closing his eyes, he tried again with a mirror image of the napkin to his lips, then watched to see if she responded.

Beluga snorted. "You've seen the worst of human conditions in your years of medical practice. Including meeting Tanya. Surely a smear of chocolate and Bavarian cream on my face can't be that bad. Just tell me where the damn thing is and let's end this."

Doc licked the end of his linen napkin and dragged it across Beluga's upper lip. "There. Are you happy? You've turned me into my mother. Do me a favor and pass on the candied ginger and cream cheese sandwiches."

"Why?"

"Because I don't have the social stamina to pry a sweetened rhizome originating from a tall, flowering plant—botanical name *Zingiber officinale*, family name *N.O. Zingiberaceae*—out from between your teeth."

"There it is!" Beluga said. "That's why I'm here."

"So that I might practice elective dental techniques, or because you're trying to make me crazy? Which is it?"

"Here's a test. What's the medicinal value of ginger root? I bet you know."

"Of course I know." Doc hesitated momentarily. "As I recall, some say it helps with dyspepsia."

"What's that?"

"Upset stomach. And it can be useful for problems with flatulence—"

"That word I understand. And that's what I'm talking about."

"Flatulence? Really, Beluga. I love you dearly, but there are some things about you I'd rather not know."

"It's not about me. Well, it's kinda about me. Let's just say I'm involved in a peripheral sort of way."

Doc nodded. "I see. You're here about a 'friend's' problem with gas. If I had a dime every time I heard that—"

"What? No. Nothing like that."

"Then it seems I'm a bit lost in this conversation."

She reached deep into the pocket of her muumuu for the plant stem. "I'm here for this."

"What is it?" he said, reaching for a pair of reading glasses from a platinum box.

"I was hoping you could tell me."

He rolled the stem over and over in his hands, then raised it to his nose for a sniff. "Wherever did you find it?"

"On the floor under the bottom shelf of a commercial freezer near a dead body."

Doc looked at her over the rim of his glasses. "Of

course you did."

"No, really. I did."

"I don't doubt it for a minute, I'm sad to say. So cooking school has rendered more than perhaps you bargained for?"

"How did you know I was in cooking school?"

He smiled. The tic in his face started up. "News of your exploits travel fast."

"Tanya."

"She rung me up just a while ago asking for the name of a fast, and cheap, caterer."

"She can squeeze a penny so hard it'll turn into a quarter."

"Yes. So I gave her the name of the most expensive caterer I know. *Quid pro quo*."

"The ugly Carmen Miranda incident at your 'Come As You Were' party?"

"No one messes with my fine Italian porcelain fruit display. No one. But that's neither here nor there." He stood up, stroked Planchette under the chin and spoke something softly into his ear which made the cat purr, then turned to Beluga. "Come with me."

She did. They set off at a rapid pace through a series of rooms that led to the kitchen, then out a set of French doors to a connecting glass-enclosed greenhouse.

Beluga's breath caught at the change in temperature. It was warm here compared to the sitting room. Hot even. Stifling. And there was enough humidity in the air to make her hair look like a well-used wire pot scrubber. She wilted in the atmosphere, unlike the dense foliage that clearly thrived and even flourished under these conditions. Sweat accumulated on her forehead and ran into her eyes.

"It's like a hothouse in here."

"Yes," Doc said. "That's the idea."

They passed the more tropical foliage, and the carnivorous plants that held prey in various forms of pre- and post-consumption, then trotted past an impressive display of rare orchids. Together they turned a corner to a newly added wing and Beluga was grateful for the dip in temperature. Here human life—hers anyway—had a chance of survival.

She couldn't help notice Doc hadn't broken into the first sign of a sweat. Honestly, men had it so easy. Whatever thermodynamic principles they were born with were what they had almost all their lives. Women, on the other hand, lived through a series of life changes that required a flexible thermostat and layered clothing at all times. It was all blatantly unfair, and she wished she knew where the counter was to register a complaint.

Doc stopped suddenly to scrutinize a flowering plant. "Speaking of rhizomes…"

Beluga dabbed at her face and knew she was beet red about now. "Were we?"

He nodded. "This is a creeping rhizome, an underground stem that sets out two leaves. See? And there, at the back of the leaves is the short flower stalk. The buds are green when they're young, then become white."

"I see that," Beluga said. She caressed a leaf, then leaned in close for a good look at the small flower stalks. "The little flowers are hanging down like bells. How pretty they are."

"And very toxic. Especially the leaves."

"What?" Beluga jumped back. "You couldn't tell

me that before I touched it?" She stared at her hand. "Is something bad going to happen? It is, isn't it?" She fanned her face. "I'm so hot. And I can't...can't...catch my...breath."

"Those are some of the symptoms of *Convallaria majalis* poisoning, that's for sure."

"Oh my God."

"Along with irritability."

"You're killing me!" she shrieked, while running around in circles.

"Hallucinations sometimes occur—"

"I should be an exotic dancer. It's my true calling."

"And in the worst cases there can be coma and death from heart failure."

Beluga slumped to the ground. "Where are you? I can't see you. Or hear anything. My time must be near. And there's so much I wanted to do." A wet cloth fell into her lap. "What's this?"

"Wipe your hands with it. You'll be fine."

"You mean I'm not dying?"

"You're not dying."

"What about the hot flash? The difficulty breathing? The irritability for Heaven's sake?"

Doc stared at her grimly. "You're in a temperature controlled greenhouse; you had a panic reaction, and at the very least you're irritating the hell out of me."

"Well, you don't have to get snippy about it."

"Snippy is the least of what you'll see if you try exotic dancing."

"I was hallucinating."

"You were fantasizing. Two very different things. For most people anyway. But do try to pay attention. This is the plant that produces the stem like the one you found in the freezer."

"*Get out!*" She popped up from the floor and looked suspiciously at the plant, this time from a calculated distance. "Really? Are you sure?"

"Pretty sure. Yes."

"What did you say the name was?"

"You may know it better as Lily of the Valley."

"Well, I'll be."

"It has been mistaken for wild garlic and used as such. Is that a possible scenario for a cause of death?"

"Yes. I suppose so," Beluga said, then corrected herself. "No. Not possible. The deceased chef, by all accounts, was an expert in these matters. Surely he would know edible garlic from a poisonous plant."

"Unless a dish was prepared for him by someone else."

Like a girlfriend scorned? Maybe.

"Anyway," Doc continued, "when not used for murder, or mistakenly described in a cookbook as a cake decoration, it has been used for medicinal purposes. Kind of a cardiac tonic. It can slow the heartbeat in people who have irritable hearts to begin with. Much like digitalis, only not as potent."

"Can it cause shortness of breath, almost the feeling of suffocation?"

"In a lethal dose. Yes. I could see that."

"Then this has to be the murder weapon."

Doc peered at her over his glasses. "Remind me again when you got your degree in forensic pathology."

"I have better credentials. Head-on, dead center, bull's eye intuition."

"You forget how long I've known you, Beluga."

"I get it right most of the time."

"Sometimes you get it right."

She chose to ignore him. "Those symptoms we just discussed are the very same that came to me at the school today, and, as you witnessed, just a while ago."

"I thought I was clear in my explanation of your so-called symptoms."

"You were. Crystal. But now I'm more clear than ever in knowing my feelings were right. That's got to count for something."

"Maybe." He stored his glasses in the platinum case, dropped it into a pocket, and steered her back through the hot zone of the greenhouse to the kitchen. "You'll need more concrete proof."

She followed his lead. Beads of perspiration popped out all over her forehead as they passed back through the hot zone.

"The murderer's confession as the result of a guilty conscience would be great, but it's not likely to happen."

"Not unless it's scripted in the last minute of a made-for-TV movie."

"Good thing I have a plan."

"You always do." His gentle yet insistent nudge to her shoulder guided her through the kitchen and further into a specially built, acoustically sound, three-story atrium.

"Holy cow on a surf board!" She gasped at the size of the room, blinked in disbelief at the massive instrument that covered one wall of the room, then fell silent at the floral displays scattered about.

"Do you like it? It's all new since the last time you were here."

Planchette appeared, a little more mellow than

when they first arrived, and curled around Doc's legs. He yawned, offered a laid back yowl, then jumped up on a writing desk that held a vase filled with roses.

At least Beluga thought they were roses. They looked like roses, but were the size of dinner plates. Steroids were in this picture, if there was such a thing for flowers, although she wouldn't overrule nuclear influences.

"I…never."

"Oh, those," he said, rather off-handedly. "Not quite as big as I hoped. Good blood is so hard to get these days."

She cocked her head. "Beg your pardon."

"Sure you can buy the dried variety at a nursery supply center, but where's the sense in that when human sacrifices are all the rage now."

"You're kidding me."

"Of course I am. I may be eccentric, but I'm not mad." The tic started anew. "At least not anymore." He reached for a single stemmed rose, inhaled deep the scent, and gave it to her. "Let's just say I have a contact at a lab. When the blood passes its expiration date and they can't use it anymore, I use it here."

"You put blood on the roses?"

"For the nitrogen. They love it."

"They are beautiful. By far the largest I've ever seen." She duly sniffed the flower, then caught sight of him from the corner of her eye. "What in the world are you doing?"

"Taking off my clothes. How do you like my organ?"

"I know you didn't just ask me that question."

"My new organ," he said, waving expansively at

the handsome instrument before him and the stately pipes that rose tall against the walls. "From an old theatre that was being renovated in Germany. A real beauty, wouldn't you say? I had to negotiate hard for this one." He took a seat on the bench.

"Must you be nude to appreciate its musical quality?"

"One can never be accused of overdressing when naked. Besides, how better to truly experience a vibrato. Care to join me?"

"I'm afraid I'll have to pass. Come along, Planchette. We have an important phone call to make, and a party to interrogate, er, attend."

With great reluctance Planchette jumped off the table. He went to Doc for one last scratch behind the ears, and if Beluga didn't know better, a snarl at her for ending his day so abruptly. He started a protracted walk toward the front door.

"We'll be back, my little familiar. I promise."

Planchette wasn't buying. The top of his tail twitched in a warning that her words better have teeth in them.

"Really. I mean it. Tell him, Doc."

"Yes, indeed. Master Planchette will be a special guest at my party. Oh, and you can come, too."

"Thanks ever so. What kind of event are you thinking about this time, Doc?"

He smiled, positioned his hands over the keys, and played a short series of deep, ominous notes from Toccata and Fugue in D Minor that filled the room and shook the house. "Perchance something to do with phantoms and operas. No clothing allowed at this affair though. Masks, however, are optional."

"Oh, dear."

Planchette pressed his nose to the front door, opened it, and walked out.

Beluga followed the feline lead. "That's my ride. Thanks for everything, Doc. See you soon I hope."

And then the concert was on. Doc sat nude and enraptured by his organ, while his guests took their leave.

Chapter 9

The party for the chef students was in full swing.

Beluga and Tanya's dorm room that morning—the very picture of a jail cell, only more austere—was this evening transformed into the inside of a desert nomad tribal tent where the denizens liked to party hearty.

Deep blue and white striped material hung in a bunch from the ceiling of the room and splayed out to the four corners, giving a feeling that was at once breath-taking and claustrophobic. And clearly wrong. This was a circus tent, not the practical black color of tents made by and lived in by people who lived in the desert. But facts never stood in the way of Tanya's plans.

Mattresses from the twin beds had been pulled to the floor and buried under large pillows, while the bed frames became disappointing trampolines for the many party attendees spilled out into the hallway. One could easily sink down, but few bounced up again.

Even that couldn't dent the festive air, for Tanya kept everyone in ample drink and food, enough for the entire county.

"Camel Dung?" Tanya offered a glass filled with a weak brown fluid to Beluga.

"Absolutely not," Beluga said. "Why would I drink such a thing, and why, may I ask, do you look like a bolt of material that's been pulled off the shelf for a fire sale?"

"Fabulous, isn't it," she said twirling around. "Imported. Pricey. And extremely original to tonight's theme."

"If tonight's theme is based on what happens when designer bed sheets get twisted in a dryer. How long did it take to put that thing on?"

"The question is, how long will it take to get out of it? I'll need a metal detector just to find all the safety pins. Still, it's not how you feel, it's how you look that counts. But you wouldn't understand." Tanya thrust the drink at Beluga. "Now have a Camel Dung and loosen up."

"Pass."

Tanya leaned in close. "It's Irish cream with a hint of club soda."

Beluga snatched it away. "Why didn't you say so in the first place?"

"Go with the theme, dear. But between us, steer clear of a drink called Dromedary Spit."

"What in the world—?"

"It's best you don't know."

"Where's the phone?" Beluga asked.

"Directory assistance won't know about the drink either. Believe me, I've already tried."

"No. I need to make a phone call."

"Oh," Tanya paused for a moment, looked around, then shrugged. "Try looking under that large drum in the corner. Or maybe it's behind the stuffed flamingo."

"Flamingoes? In the nomadic desert?"

"Last minute event, remember. We do what we can. I love creative interior decorators who owe me a favor, don't you? Anyway, the phone is around here somewhere."

"Thanks. I'll give it a shot." Beluga found the phone eventually, but not in either of the places to which she was directed or in the form it took when she found it. She plunked down on a large pillow, sure she'd never get up again without emergency assistance, dialed the number, waited, then shouted over the din when he answered. "Darwin? It's me. Beluga."

A pause.

"Darwin. Please. I'm calling you from a phone shaped like a hookah so don't push me. What's that? Yes. You heard me correctly. A hookah." She nodded, rolled her eyes, sipped Camel Dung from a plastic cup bearing the long-faced, distinctly unhappy demeanor of a tiki god, then interrupted him. "Darwin, for just a moment, try to put aside your theories on my Bohemian-like lifestyle. And do not even *think* about arguing with my unwavering disinterest in gumming a phone to my body twenty-four-seven, regardless of its Lilliputian characteristics. Now listen to me... What's that? No, dear. The hookah is not mine, it's Tanya's." She pulled the phone from her ear and grimaced at the screech coming from the other end.

"Darwin... Darwin. Would that I could corrupt Tanya, but it seems she's perfectly capable of that all by herself. It's rented, dear. That's right. The hookah's rented, along with just about everything else. For the party we're having. An interrogation party, really. Although I must say that information has yet to be forthcoming. And that's where you come in."

Another screech.

Beluga held the phone at bay until the sound subsided. "Darwin, darling, you really must take a page

83

from your father's medical history and learn to calm yourself lest you, too, turn into a walking knot with high blood pressure. By the way, how is the dear M.E.? One expects he misses me terribly."

Beluga extended the phone again and massaged her temple. "That was a rather rude noise. One hopes it's not a direct quote. Was it now? Well, you can tell your father from me he got off easy. It was just a nip really. Hardly noticeable at all for a goat chomp. And a good thing Emerson's bark is worse than his bite especially considering the unfortunate location of the wound." She rubbed her backside in an act of sympathy pain. "But, and I use that term carefully, your father should consider the event a matter of professional courtesy from one old goat to another. Write that down, Darwin. I want to make sure you get it word for word. What's that? Oh, yes. The reason for my call. What do you know about Lily of the Valley?"

She took another sip of Camel Dung, waved at Tanya for a refill, then snorted into the phone. "Beside the fact it would be a great name for an exotic dancer. Honestly, Darwin, with your mind in the gutter like that, how do you have room to learn anything in medical school? Never mind the tirade, I'm working up one of my own if you don't settle down and listen. So here's the deal. You should be in receipt of a body by the name of John Doe."

Tanya handed over a plastic champagne flute filled with a lethal-looking, neon green concoction.

Beluga waved it away. "Yes, that's his real name. Yes, I know it can be a common name in the M.E.'s office, but the circumstance of his death is far from common, and I would be eternally grateful if you looked into it."

Tanya pushed the flute closer.

Beluga glared at Tonya, then shook her head. "I discovered his body in a commercial freezer at cooking school. Yes, a freezer. Why?" Her eyes narrowed to slits. "Laughing at my situation is most unbecoming, dear heart."

Tanya stamped her foot and lunged the drink.

"Hold on, Darwin. I need a sec to address a pest control issue." Beluga eyed the drink suspiciously, then turned the same look on Tanya. "What happened to the Camel Dung?"

"All out. Ditto Gonad Goo, Humpback Hooch, and something I think will put you in a coma almost instantly called 'Here's Sand In Your Eye.' Chef students are nothing if not disturbingly artistic."

"What is it?"

"Drink. Don't ask. And don't go looking for a lampshade to put on your head. They're all being used right now." Tanya sighed, forced a smile then turned on her heel—a shroud of wrinkled material disappearing among a throng of delighted party guests.

Beluga sniffed the drink, took a tentative sip, then spluttered it out across the front of her muumuu. "Great ghosts among us, that's Dromedary Spit! What? No, no, Darwin. That was not a slam on your person or your many fine merits. I was referring to a nasty cocktail."

She handed the glass to a random passerby who accepted it, then watched the willing victim down the drink in one swift motion. From the looks of her, this wasn't the first Dromedary Spit Jackleg had consumed tonight.

Beluga studied Jackleg sway to a beat perhaps only

she could hear, and adopt a small introspective smile perhaps to a story only she could know. Without warning Jackleg collapsed into the lotus position on a pillow next to Beluga. She leaned in until their noses just touched, attempted an unsuccessful wink that involved every muscle in her face, and uttered a series of guttural noises until they finally found form with recognizable words. "I know something you don't know. Something no one knows."

"Do you now?"

The young woman bobbed her head in a slow deliberate motion that went from star-gazing to chin on chest. "It's about Chef Doe."

Beluga's eyebrows rose a notch. She raised a "just a second" finger to hold Jackleg's further information reveal, then turned to whisper into the phone, "Darwin, listen. An opportunity might have opened up here and I'd better take it." She turned back to Jackleg, raised the finger again, then returned to the phone. "Look into John Doe for me, will you? And keep in mind poisoning by a plant called Lily of the Valley. Yes, I know you're only a medical student. Yes, I know you only work part time at your dad's office. Yes, I know about body parts in a sling if this gets ugly. Just do it. Please. And get back to me. Love and kisses. Double to your father. Tell him to call me. Bye-bye."

The hookah was reassembled as best Beluga could figure, and now she was ready to test out her questioning skills on the bleary-eyed questionee. "So Jack—uh, Jeanette. You knew—"

"Jack. Yeah. Of course, I knew him. Knew him as Jackie-boy. Jack-o-lantern. The Jackmeister. That was one piece of work if you ask me."

"Really?"

"Oh, yeah. If you only knew the half of it."

"I'd be more than happy to know it all."

"I've been sworn to secrecy." She tried winking again, but gave up mid-muscle spasm.

"Secrecy, huh? We'll see about that. Tanya!" Beluga bellowed. "A Dromedary Spit for my friend here. And be quick about it."

"That's a really good drink. I mean rockin' good. You gonna have one?" She leaned heavily against Beluga's shoulder and breathed fetid odors at her. "I don't like to drink alone, you know."

Beluga swallowed dryly and squeaked the order. "Make it two, please."

Jackleg patted Beluga on the knee with every spoken word. "You. Are. All. Right."

That clenched it. If not for the alcohol, there's no way on heaven and earth this girl would consider Beluga "all right." It simply wasn't in Jackleg's nature, and if Beluga consulted them she knew it wouldn't be in the tarot cards either.

Pushing the need for information aside, Beluga's protective instincts suddenly kicked in. "Maybe you've had enough."

"No. No. No," she said, patting Beluga's knee with growing insistence. "I'm fine. I. Am. Perfectly. Fine."

"We've got a busy day in the kitchen tomorrow."

"Good. To. Go. That's. Me."

The words came to Beluga then. Not words of her own making, but words that emerged from a source outside herself. Or deep within her intuitive senses. "You've got to stay on your toes if you want to make it in this world."

The patting stopped mid-air. A stricken look formed in Jackleg's eyes, followed by an onrush of tears. "That's what he always said."

"Who? And remind me again what I just said. It just kinda popped out, and my short term memory isn't what it used to be."

"*Him*. He said that."

"Chef Doe?"

"And I hated him for it."

"You hated him?"

"Yes. No." Jackleg wiped her eyes. "Sometimes."

"Hi, everyone." Katie Cliff's sing-song voice punctured the air.

"Not now," Beluga said waving her away.

"Two Dromedary Spits just the way you ordered them. And a pineapple juice for me. I'm not one for the evils of alcohol, you know." Katie wedged a tray with the drinks between Beluga and Jackleg. "Or any kind of evil for that matter. Unless it's justified, of course."

Beluga stared at her.

"Just kidding!" Katie covered her mouth and giggled. "You should have seen the look on your face. It was great." The look on her face immediately shifted to one of concern and a little worry. "Say, how do you think I'm doing in school so far? I think everyone likes me. Don't you think everyone likes me? I think they do. I like everyone in class. And it's so fun."

"Yes," Beluga said without enthusiasm. "You're doing fine. Everyone is in a heightened state of liking one another. Fun. Blah, blah, blah." She eyed Jackleg, who looked with lust at the Dromedary Spit, but was having difficulty with the needed motor skills to retrieve it from the tray. "Tanya couldn't bring the

88

drinks herself and then leave quickly and discreetly? If you get my drift."

"Tanya told me to bring them. She's the best, isn't she? Such an interesting conversationalist and in so many languages."

"English not being among them," Beluga muttered under her breath.

"And her outfit! I just love her outfit," Katie gushed. "So what are you two talking about?"

Jackleg finally captured the drink.

Beluga pulled it away from her. "No more. You're cut off." Then she saw the veritable garden that sat on the rim of the glass. "What's all that?"

"Mesclun," Jackleg said peering myopically at the glass. "Mizuna, frisee, purslane, calendulas." A single tear rolled down her face. Her voice broke. "And bachelor's buttons."

"Festive, isn't it?" Katie piped up. "All of it looks so nice. What did you call it again?"

Jackleg reached for the glass in Beluga's hand and the two pulled an immediate stalemate in their tug-of-war. "Mesclun."

"Mesclun?" Katie said. "I've never heard of that before."

"How do you know so much about, you know, greenery?" Beluga asked Jackleg while fighting to keep control of the glass without a drop being spilled.

Jackleg shrugged. "I guess... because... because..." Her eyes suddenly rolled up into her head. She released the glass, fell back entangled in the hookah, and passed out to the sound of a dial tone.

Beluga did not fare as well. One Dromedary Spit spilled across the tray and saturated the lap of her muumuu. The other, upon release of tightly held tension, spewed its contents volcano-like high into the air and came down over her head like a waterfall.

"Ooh," Katie Cliff said, snatching up her intact glass of pineapple juice while backing away from the mêlée. "That's a shame. But at least I saved my juice."

Now a new voice broke the air with a booming, "*What's this*?" And the great Ned Niblett was before them, filling the doorway.

Katie jumped, tossed away her pineapple juice on the one remaining dry place on Beluga's muumuu, and made herself very small to skitter away with the rest of the students like cockroaches when a light comes on.

The silence was heavy with tension.

"Chef Niblett," she said, rolling over on her belly. Using all available limbs and joints, she thrust her backside high in the air, then pushed herself up to stand in some semblance of *homo erectus*. "So kind of you to drop by. Have you been introduced to my friend, Tanya?"

"Nice to meet you, Ned." Tanya smiled broadly, cocked her hip in a come-hither stance and thrust out her hand.

He ignored the offer of a handshake and familiarity. "I am a professional."

"I'm sure." The smile turned rigid on her face. She withdrew her hand and glared. "Clearly the pleasure, if there were any, would be all mine."

Jackleg moaned, then curled up in a fetal position.

"And," Beluga said with a wave of her hand, "I trust you know Miss Mason."

"Clean this up," Ned Niblett said simply. "Now."

"Of course. We'll be happy to. Won't we, Tanya?"

"Not on your—"

"And there you have it," Beluga said. "See? Consider it done."

The chef scrutinized the room as if making sure every detail was permanently seared in his mind. Minutes passed in what felt like hours until he spoke again. "My office. Six o'clock sharp." He backed out of the room with a final glance, and turned away.

"Excuse me," Beluga said with a catch in her throat.

Ned Niblett stopped without benefit of looking at her.

"One hopes that when you say six, you are referring to the more acceptable evening hour."

His back stiffened.

"I mean, otherwise that's only a short time from now and I'm really not a morning person."

"Trust me," Tanya piped up, "she's not kidding one bit. I, on the other hand, can look refreshed and becoming any time of the day or night."

"Yeah," Beluga said. "If you've got that tackle box you call a make-up bag with you, a beauty consultant on twenty-four-hour call, and a sidecar iced and ready for consumption."

Tanya snorted. "See what I mean, Ned, er, Chef. Since it's a matter of personal safety to only imagine her personality at the crack of dawn, you may want to reconsider the appointment schedule."

"*Six. Both of you.*"

"Not me, too?" She looked at Beluga. "I know he doesn't mean me. I had nothing to do with this."

"You had everything to do with this."

"Only because you weren't getting anywhere on

the case since everyone hates you."

"They don't hate me. And who said it was a case?"

"It is a case and you know it. Otherwise why would you call Darwin?"

"To see if it's a case."

"Well? Is it?"

"It might be," Beluga conceded. "Yeah. I'm almost certain it is."

"Then it's your case and I will not be a party to it. It's settled, Ned. I mean, Chef. Beluga will be in your office at six, and I will take the day off. Chef?" Tanya looked out the door. "Chef?" She came back into the room. "I hope you're happy. He's gone."

"So you and me. Six. Which by my calculations is," she looked at her arm where a watch would be if she wore one, "not near enough time to clean up, get some sleep, and meet in his office."

"*Perilamvani ke proyevma*? Is breakfast included?"

"I wouldn't count on it. I'm guessing more a lecture du jour as opposed to eggs, biscuits, and country ham."

"Say, that does sound good." Tanya dropped down onto an overstuffed pillow near a lidded rope basket. "What do you say we go to the kitchen and rustle up some home cooking?"

"Yeah, sure," Beluga said, poking around under decorative accessories and wads of material. "By the time you bring the wagon train around, I'll have those rustled up made-from-scratch biscuits just begging for some of my fresh homemade butter, not to mention the honey I squeezed from the bees themselves. Where is Planchette? I haven't seen him since we got back from Doc's place."

"It was just a thought."

"Well, think again. I can't even make biscuits from a can, and you know how I am with eggs. Besides, the kitchen is locked."

Tanya picked at a loose end on the side of the lidded rope basket. "How do you know?"

Beluga paused then. "I guess I assumed the kitchen was locked. I mean, why wouldn't it be?"

"Why would it be?"

"Because there's stuff in there. Expensive equipment, food, supplies. Stuff like that. And it stops people like us from getting into more trouble."

"The meeting's at six. And a lecture is a lecture. So what if it's a longer, more heated lecture by virtue of an unsupervised kitchen expedition?" Tanya flicked another loose end that stuck out from the basket and watched with a raised eyebrow as it disappeared.

"Planchette? Where are you, boy?"

Just as suddenly as the loose end had vanished, it reappeared. Tanya grabbed it and pulled.

A high-pitched shriek pierced the air. The top of the basket bounced upward, then fell back askew on the rim.

"I think I've discovered the whereabouts of your familiar."

Beluga tipped the basket lid, waited a couple of seconds, then a handsome, yet cautious feline face emerged from the dark depths. Green eyes scanned the room for overzealous party guests.

"It's okay, my little love. It's just me and Auntie Tanya. You're safe now."

He hesitated. Then with the sound of claws finding purchase, he oozed himself from the basket and into

Beluga's arms.

"What in the world?" Cradling him in the crook of one elbow, she stared at the motif of palm trees and fallen coconuts on a vivid green background that clothed him from his neck to the base of his tail. "Why is my cat wearing a Hawaiian shirt?"

Tanya suddenly found deep interest in her fingernails. "I don't know."

"No idea, huh?" Beluga asked, while pulling the offending material from his taut body and tossing it at Tanya.

"None. Sorry."

"There now," she cooed to Planchette. "All better." She nuzzled his face and ran her hand in long strokes down his sleek body. "No one can improve on perfection. That's what I always say."

A purr started deep in his throat. His claws emerged and retracted in a satisfied rhythm. He closed his eyes.

"You're safe with me, Planchette," she whispered in his ear. "But if you feel the urge to turn Auntie Tanya into confetti I won't stop you."

"I had nothing to do with the basket. You should know that. He found that hiding place all by himself."

One feline eye popped open to stare at his nemesis.

"Tell her, Planchette," Tanya said. "Tell her I'm speaking the truth."

Planchette yawned and adopted a look of practiced boredom.

She snarled then. "I should have known you'd take Beluga's side. You always take her side. No one ever takes my side."

"Turn around," Beluga said. "Which side shall I

take? The large one or the larger one?"

"Very funny. And totally uncalled for."

"Uncalled for? I'll tell you what's uncalled for. The way you treated him."

Planchette rolled out of her arms and landed squarely on his feet. Frozen. Unmoving. Watchful.

"He's a cat," Tanya said, with a dismissive wave in his general direction.

"And you're an animal."

"I beg your pardon."

"Beg all you want. It doesn't change the facts. *Hawaiian shirts*? What's next? Sports attire? Tuxedoes?"

"If the party theme fits…"

A low growl emerged from deep in the cat's throat.

Beluga jabbed a finger at Tanya's chest. "I'll show you where you can put your party theme."

Tanya jabbed back. "And I'll show you that I don't need this anymore."

"Show me." *Jab.*

"I will." *Jab.*

"I'm waiting." *Jab.*

"Well, you can just wait until I'm good and ready." *Jab. Jab.*

Planchette hissed. Every hair on his body stood on end effectively making him twice the cat he normally was.

Beluga and Tanya watched him back away, eyes wide, unblinking, and staring at something near the door.

As if they were two figurines atop a lazy susan, the two women turned in tandem to see what had captured the cat's unbroken attention.

"Do you see anything," Tanya asked.

"No. Do you?"

"I'm afraid if I look too hard I might."

"Planchette sees something."

"That does it," Tanya said. "Now I'm just afraid."

"What is it, boy?"

Mere inches off the ground, Planchette skulked toward the door. The tip of his tail twitched. One foot tentatively followed another. Ears folded back on his head, he approached the door and slowly looked left.

"I guess everything's okay?" Tanya asked.

"No."

"Please tell me that whatever it is, it's gone now."

"I don't think so."

"I'm begging you, Beluga. Pleading, really. I'll even get on my knees and—"

Slowly, ever so slowly, Planchette stood in the doorway and this time he looked right.

A laugh sounded. Quiet. Almost subliminal. But unmistakable nonetheless.

And then there it was. Or rather, there *he* was. Short—three feet at best—a malicious glimmer in his eyes, he lunged forward and was at once by Planchette's side.

The cat leapt straight up in the air. Like a shot he was gone, with a laughing little man following close at his heels.

"Planchette!" Beluga screamed.

"I saw it." Tanya ran in tight circles while covering her face. "My eyes! My eyes! May I never see anything like that again." She stopped and jabbed Beluga in the chest. "And you can't make me."

"Then stay here. I'm going after Planchette."

"And leave me here with God knows what? Not on your life. Lead on."

"Planchette," Beluga yelled, as she ran out the door and down the hall. "Hang on, boy. I'm coming."

Chapter 10

Beluga ran for all she was worth. Through the dorm hallway that was all but abandoned save for an occasional eye that peeped around an open door to watch, then down a flight of stairs, and another.

Ahead of her was the more and more elusive glimpse of Planchette's tail and the hair-raising laugh from a sinister shadow that stayed hot on his heels.

Following Beluga was an expletive-spewing, huffing and puffing, drawn out melodramatic wheezing Tanya. The sequence of sounds she produced were less than joyous in this time of pursuit, perhaps they were even painful, but if put together Beluga could almost glean a disjointed commentary on, what was it, attire? Was Tanya really worried about destroying her party fashion choice while pursuing Planchette?

"*Werg ug gonig. Sto...stog...ese.*"

"Plenty of time to talk later."

There were also plenty more tacky materials where Tanya had found the first bolt, so sympathy for her perceived tragedy could wait. Much bigger concerns lay ahead, and time was wasting to save Planchette from whatever diabolical scheme the strange little man had in mind.

It had to be diabolical. Just had to be. His gleeful laugh made it so. His sudden visibility to the naked eye clinched it. But what exactly he was, why he was here, and what he planned to do was just as mysterious right now as the whereabouts of her cat.

She arrived breathless at a door at the bottom of the stairwell and turned the knob. It stayed frozen in place, whether turned clockwise or counterclockwise. And yet, there was no other way out, no place to go from here but back up where surely she would have passed her cat and the little man.

"Planchette! Where are you?"

A scuttling sounded outside the door. Then came a yowl that faded with distance from ongoing escape.

That did it. If the door knob wouldn't turn she would have to come up with another plan. Something with immediate results. And then she had it, ramming speed. Bending low, she tensed one shoulder to accept the brunt of a splintering impact if that's what was called for. Clearly there was no other way.

Except for the unexpected series of events that were even now forming behind her.

"Oh-oh-oh. Wat...ow!" Tanya stumbled a step, missed three more, and for a moment, against all known physical law and perhaps even veteran Las Vegas odds makers, she became airborne and possibly gravity-free. "Gon...hur..."

But in this world of physical law, weightlessness was not to be. Gravity, instead, was the painful victor.

The impact of the two women was solid, convincing, and extremely effective. The door never stood a chance. It swung open almost effortlessly, to spill two flailing bodies into a heap on the floor of the main lobby.

It was in that instant Beluga found herself caught between releasing a breath and never being able to accept one again. The collision knocked her into total darkness and an almost welcomed senselessness that warranted looking for the light, going into the light for the next adventure, and if necessary chasing the damn light to go into it. For she had to be dead, if not on a slippery water slide to dying. The weight upon her was all but dead, so surely the light would appear at any time.

Then it did.

Tanya moved her arm from across Beluga's eyes, and the glare from perpetually lit fluorescent bulbs flooded her retinas.

"I…can't…breathe."

"I can. Finally." Tanya said, rolling off Beluga. "Thank God you broke my fall, or I'd be sipping Champagne through a straw. Which, by the way, can be kind of fun under the right circumstances."

"The door."

Tanya pulled herself up and looked. "Yup. Looks like it was oiled recently. A committed push would have opened it, but I'd say what we did was a lot more colorful if not infinitely more exciting. Are you okay?"

"Never better." Beluga groaned. "Now that you're off my back."

An elongated, two-note feline threat sounded from around the corner in the dining room.

"Help me up, Tanya," she said, holding out a hand. "I think I've twisted my knee, and we gotta get Planchette."

"I don't know. He sounds mad, like he might have something cornered. Maybe it's best if we wait things out."

"No. No waiting. Help me up, or I'll bite you in the

shin. I can do it, too."

"Honestly. You can be so single-minded sometimes." Tanya pulled, tugged, yanked, and finally wrenched Beluga to a stand.

Beluga moaned and rubbed the swelling that was already starting in her knee. "Lead on. I'll be right behind you."

"No, no. Oh, absolutely no. I'm not going to be the first one to arrive at the scene. There's no telling what I'll see."

"Fine. Have it your way." Beluga limped toward the corner that turned to the dining room and the kitchen. "And best of luck to you next time you need help with a problematic ghost. Or an invitation to an exclusive party."

"Coming through!" Tanya yelled. Loping down the hallway, she cleared the corner and covered her eyes. "Don't scare me. Please, whatever you are, don't scare me."

Staggering along, Beluga finally caught up to them in the dining room. Planchette's fur stood out as if he had been newly washed and blown dry. He pawed at the door to the kitchen while uttering a subtle, but intent growl deep in his throat.

Tanya stood a short distance away from the cat with her hands against the glass window and cupped around the sides of her face so she could get a better look into the dark kitchen. "You will be glad to know," she said, stare never wavering, "you were right."

"Aren't I always?"

"Seldom, dear. Seldom. But you were right this time in that the kitchen is locked. And trust me when I tell you how happy that news makes me."

"How so?"

After stepping back from the glass, Tanya adjusted her party attire into some semblance of decency and waved Beluga to the window. "See for yourself."

"What is it?"

"Hard to tell, really. But it doesn't look good."

"I see." Beluga squinted at the glass and the kitchen beyond. "No, I can't say I see anything at all."

"Look again."

It was dark in there. Dark as a tomb. But as her vision adjusted she began to see a little something. The blue-white pilot lights flickered within each eye of the many stoves and in the back of broilers. Small rectangular slivers of red lights proved the refrigerators and freezers, reach-ins and walk-ins, were working.

And then there was something else.

She strained harder, focused, concentrated with every bit of energy she had on the shadow within shadow movement in the kitchen until—

Crash!

Beluga jumped back. "What was that?"

"I have no idea," Tanya said, with an unusual calmness in her voice. "But here's an interesting twist." She waved her hand across the spider cracks on the glass as if she were turning a vowel in a game show.

"The little man from upstairs? The one who chased Planchette down here? Did he throw something at me?"

"No earthly idea at all."

No earthly idea indeed. If not who he was, Beluga now knew at least what he was. Fairly sure anyway. Well, pretty certain. It was better than a hunch. Yeah. Her intuition said she was on the right track so she decided there was nothing left but to go with it.

"You'll be glad to know you're right, Tanya."

"How so?"

"He's not one of us, that's for sure. But of this earth? I'm betting on it. Old Earth. Very old. And from what I've read, it's pretty rare that any of us actually get to see one like him."

More breaking glass came from the kitchen.

"Although hearing them doesn't seem to be a problem. Planchette! I'm in need of your skills."

The cat leapt to full attention.

"What are you doing?" Tanya asked.

"I'm going in."

"You're what?"

"Going in. To the kitchen."

"I told you. The door is locked."

"There has to be another way in. Planchette, that morning when we discovered Chef Doe…"

His tail twitched.

"Try to remember how you got out, and we'll go in that way. Can you do it, boy?"

He licked a paw, hesitated a moment.

"Take me there. But don't go too fast. Bum knee."

Planchette turned, looked back over his shoulder at her, and broke into a slow trot toward the far end of the dining room.

Tanya shooed them. "I'll take a pass this time, if you don't mind."

Beluga nodded, then limped after the cat. "Good plan, dear friend. Keep an eye on things and sound an alarm if danger rears its ugly head."

"Yeah, yeah," Tanya said, settling into a chair for the long haul. "Danger. Keep an eye out. Ugly headed events. It's all part of the job when I'm with you."

"You're the best."

"Whatever."

"Okay, Planchette. Lead on."

They stopped at a small door just past the kitchen. Locked. The next door was locked just the same. The third door rattled a little when touched, then opened.

"Bingo!"

She flipped a light switch that cast a dull yellow from bulbs badly needing replacement and saw they were in a conference room. This room was probably much like the other locked ones, but there was no way out of here except from whence they came.

Planchette glanced around the room and went to a wall for a sniff. No way out unless...sure. That was it. This room could expand its accommodation space by a simple slide of a divider wall.

Or a not so simple slide Beluga discovered when she tried pushing it. It wobbled, but stood firm.

"So what's next?"

A single *meow* arose from the cat, followed by a roll of his green eyes.

"Turn the lock. Of course. What would I do without you?"

She twisted the bar, released the hold on the fan-fold divider wall that shot opened as if it were on a coiled spring, and the two walked in. There, on a far wall in the other room, was a door. The very door where Ned Niblett had made his sweeping entrance during the orientation session.

And it was wide open.

"Okay, boy. This is it. Or it might be it. Let's see what happens, shall we?"

The yellow glow from aging bulbs gave up the

ghost then, and Beluga had to rely on other methods of geographical positioning. Traversing the room crab-like, she waved her arms in front of her to avoid a disagreeable and unexpected encounter with an unmovable object. A concussion was the last thing on her to-do list right now. Second to last was living her life with a face designed by Picasso.

Fortunately, luck was with her this time. She touched a wall and could relax that the last two things on her to-do list were checked off.

But as luck was wont to do, it ran out all too soon. Fumbling about in the hopes of locating another light switch, she found none, and with a deep breath held, she crossed the threshold from a dark room into a darker hallway.

It was much cooler here, almost damp, with a hint of chemical cleaners in the air. Something grazed her ankle. She stumbled away from it, fell sideways against what seemed to be a large bin that clattered enough to make plates crack, then recovered herself enough to decide a smoke would be just the thing to calm her nerves.

Of course. Why hadn't she thought of it before? She dug deep into the pocket of her muumuu, bypassed the pastel cigarettes for something far more immediate to this cause, and held it aloft. The small flame from the lighter cast a shallow glow in the crowded, narrow hallway, but it might be enough to prevent a fracture or that dreaded Picasso look. Too bad she couldn't say the same for the stack of dishes she had crashed into. The top ones, at least, had not fared well.

Swinging the lighter around, she stepped carefully past all sorts of storage paraphernalia. There were the broken dishes now behind her, stacks of folding chairs here, folded tables that leaned against the wall over there, and shelves covered with all sorts of baking pans in a myriad of shapes.

The flame grew hot against her finger. She released the lever and allowed herself to be consumed into a total black. It was dark enough in here, tight enough, quiet enough, that if she barely tried, she could hear her knee swell and her heart beat. Well, if nothing else she hoped that meant her body was still at least partially working.

She blew on the lighter, flicked it to flame again, and swung it about like a bad actor playing a reluctant rookie cop holding an unfamiliar gun in a bad movie. A pass here—bins of eating utensils—a sweep there—an army of stainless rolling carts covered with lethal looking equipment lined up like little robots—over there, a pair of glowing eyes, and next to that—

Eyes?

Glowing eyes?

Her shriek punctured the air and sent ear-bleeding echoes down the hallway. The lighter dropped to the floor and went out. She bent over for it and cracked her head on a cart. A sudden spasm in her bad knee made her foot kick out, sending the fallen lighter scuttling away to a place where no doubt it would never be found again.

"Great Goddess among us, Planchette. You scared me half to death."

Silky soft fur caressed her ankles.

"Apology accepted. Remarkable as your eyes are, I prefer to adore them with a light source. Although that doesn't seem immediately likely." She rubbed what would be an impressive goose egg on her forehead and took a tentative step. "At least that crack on my head has made me see stars. Perhaps I can use them as a means of navigation." Her bum knee grazed a utility shelf, toppled a bottle of a particularly odiferous solution, and she released a most unladylike expletive. "So much for sailors and their stars. I want light, and I want it now."

And then there *was* light.

Of sorts.

A bottle rolled into the hallway from an adjoining space. Captured in the glass was a light, or rather what seemed a reflection of light from something just ahead and partially around the bend.

Around the bend. She snorted at how appropriate that thought described her current condition. Still, there was a mission to complete. A deep wallow in self-pity and a recuperation from her many collected wounds would have to wait. Right now there were discoveries to be made, a case to be solved, and more importantly, a self-serving, imperative need to make the hair on her neck and arms stand down from their alert position. The kitchen was just around that bend, and therein was the source of her wariness.

A second bottle clattered to the floor, rolled aimlessly, then stopped against a wall she had just discovered via an intimate part of her chest anatomy. Breasts as global positioning devices, who knew? But now was not the time to dwell on the potential for biological signaling equipment when other more important matters were at hand.

Adopting her best surprise stance, she launched herself into the back hallway of the kitchen and landed flat-footed, feet wide apart, and body as low to the ground as her girth would allow, while uttering a single, high-pitched "Hi-yah!."

Nothing. Not a single attacker anywhere in sight. And while she felt some relief that she had skirted possible bodily harm, there was also a little disappointment that her "hi-yah" was wasted in what might otherwise have been an entirely appropriate situation. Rare indeed was it when one got to use such tactics and language.

Another crash sounded disturbingly close by and pulled her to an upright stance like a marionette yanked by tight strings. In one sweeping gesture she grazed the wall, hit a switch, and threw the kitchen into all its illuminated glory. And in those first seconds of illumination she caught sight of him again; the little man.

He was less than three feet tall, she saw. Decidedly less.

Clothed in attire that looked homespun, he swayed unsteadily on his feet, attempted blood-shot eye contact, belched deeply, then distracted her with a shrug of his shoulders and a nod that someone else had arrived and was even at this moment standing behind her.

She snatched a fleeting glance over her shoulder, saw nothing there, and returned her gaze to the little man who had completely disappeared. "Where… How…? Well, I'll be damned."

"Yes, ma'am," a voice said. "And that might be the least of your problems when the chef hears about this mess." The night security guard stepped out of the shadows of the back hallway to reveal himself.

He was tall, imposing, and his sudden appearance scared what was left of daylights out of Beluga. But she sensed kindness in him, too. And patience.

"Yours?" he asked, passing the now docile Planchette over to her.

"Yes. Thank you." She held the cat close to her chest as if his nearness could slow her pounding heartbeat. "What a night we've had."

"So I see," he said, eyeing her Dromedary Spit-soaked attire. He nudged an empty liquor bottle with his foot. "I'm one for a drink now and then myself. Won't deny it. Look forward to it in fact, after a long day. Single malts are a particular favorite—"

"From Scotland."

"No place does better. But I would never think of taking another man's liquor. Especially if it comes from a locked cabinet."

"You don't think I did this, do you?"

"I know what I see, ma'am."

Beluga blustered and waved expansively at the sea of bottles that covered the floor. Most were empty, but a few still held enough for a snort or two. "Not on my best day in college could I have even made an alcohol dent like this. Even if I were in a fraternity I couldn't do this. Not that I didn't try, mind you. Joining a fraternity, I mean. In this day and age do we really need more gender barriers? I think not."

"Perhaps not," the guard conceded. "I wouldn't know about that. But you threw a party last night that might have needed additional, uh, beverage enhancements."

She stared at him. "How do you know about the party?"

"Well—"

"Or, for that matter, that I was in the kitchen?"

A violent rapping sounded on the observation glass to the kitchen. Beluga stepped further into the room and saw a frantic Tanya stare at her knuckles, chew a ragged fingernail, wince, and rap again. Thus began the game of Charades wherein Tanya tried to mime to Beluga that danger was lurking nearby and might at any time rear its ugly head. Tanya's last effort in this game was an improvisation of a nightstick landing repeatedly in her palm while she walked stiffly about.

Beluga almost imperceptibly shook her head no.

Tanya caught the expression, grimaced, and resorted to the only thing left she could apparently think of which was to put an imaginary noose around her neck and yank. Her tongue lolled from the corner of her mouth for a split second, followed by a gesture that if accompanied by words would have been "ta-da."

Beluga nodded, then pulled the security guard over so that her best friend would get a solid look.

The look was indeed solid. A frozen, forced smile settled on Tanya's face as she mimed walking down stairs until she disappeared from view all together.

"Your lookout?" the security guard asked.

"It seemed the best idea at the time."

"She's not very good at it."

"No. I see that now. Although she's exhibited a talent for mime I never knew she had before tonight." Beluga turned to the night security guard and peered at his name tag. "Mr. uh, Blanchard, is it?"

"Bob Blanchard, yes, ma'am. That's me."

"Am I to be arrested?"

"I'm afraid that's not my call to make, ma'am."

"But it would be a call on Ned Niblett's part?"

"That's correct."

"I figured as much," she mumbled.

"He told me to keep an eye on you after he discovered your party, and that's what I did. Followed you clear into the kitchen and found all this."

"I can explain. Really. Well, kinda. It's just that most people might find the explanation, well, rather extraordinary and perhaps a little far-fetched."

"No explanation necessary, ma'am."

"Really?" She lowered Planchette to the floor. "That's awfully kind of you, Mr. Blanchard. So I and my companion here will take up no more of your time. Good night."

He cleared his throat then. "I think you may have misunderstood me, ma'am."

Damn. So much for trying to slide by.

"I do not require an explanation, ma'am."

"But the chef does. You're assigned to see me to Ned Niblett's office, right?"

"With a full report of your activities since the party. Yes, ma'am."

"I don't suppose you'd be willing to fudge the report just a little, would you?"

"No, ma'am."

"Didn't think so."

He glanced about the disaster of half-consumed and broken bottles all over the floor. "I wouldn't begin to know how anyway. A mess such as this."

She sighed deeply. "Well, Planchette, I guess we're in it now."

Planchette scratched an ear, then yawned.

"Lead on, Mr. Blanchard. It's time to face the

music. But don't be surprised if I have a few extra notes up my sleeve."

Chapter 11

Ned Niblett never slept. He never closed an eye to rest. And some swore he never blinked.

Or so it seemed.

A total lack of sleep would at least explain his stony gaze. Beluga flipped through a culinary magazine in the waiting room outside the chef's office. She watched the dance of light and shadow under the door and guessed he was a pacer when it came to "people" decisions. But give the guy raw vegetables, meat, heat, a little Kosher salt and freshly ground pepper, and he became an artist. So the rumors said. Beluga had not yet experienced the magic, but she hoped to one day.

She blinked against dry eyes and the disturbing waft of stale Dromedary Spit on her synthetic muumuu, then stifled the urge to curl up in the waiting room chair for a little catnap. Unfortunately Planchette had beat her to a snooze and was even now resting comfortably in her lap. Beluga didn't have the heart to wake him, so she was left with no choice other than to while away the time watching the tireless dance of shadow and light under the chef's office door. The more he paced the more she wondered about the man.

Lack of sleep and people skills could be reason enough for Ned Niblett's humorless manner. Those things alone could turn anyone into a world class grouch. Perhaps he was also lonely and needed a special someone. Kind of a tragic two birds, one stone scenario.

She yawned and pondered the wonderful state of sleep—something she dearly missed right now on the eve of this coming dawn—and how lucky she was to have a special friend, however on and off. If she allowed herself to drift deep into her mind, she could remember what it was like to have sleep and him again.

There was no better place in the world to be than tucked comfortably in her bed under a pile of soft blankets. Warmth would surround her like a caress while Planchette snored softly nestled in the crook of her body. Emerson would dream of food, chew in his sleep, and shift position on his sleeping pallet that sat on the floor next to her bed. If a light rain pattered the roof, well, so much the better. All of this brought a peace to her she rarely found any other time or in any other place. And all of this brought a welcomed quiet in the middle of chaos, misunderstanding, and murder.

She closed her eyes for just a moment, and dreamed of her bed. The warmth came and surrounded her and then a hand—distinctly male—touched her shoulder and softly traveled the length of her spine. A smile of recognition followed at the touch that finally returned after being missed for so long. Too long. A deep satisfying breath came then. She turned to him, whispered his abbreviated title rather than his name, and opened her eyes…

Tanya's face loomed large and near enough that Beluga could count pores.

Beluga screamed.

Planchette shrieked and leapt off her lap.

"My thoughts exactly," Tanya said, leaning back in

her chair. "Some fine mess, huh? The security guard insisted I need to join you here in the outer sanctum of hell to await our fate. I'm betting bungee-jumping and hang gliding suddenly sound pretty good about now. And don't think I won't remind you every chance I get."

"You just took a few years off my life. Thank you very much."

Tanya leered and winked. "Maybe. But I'm guessing your last few minutes of daydreaming made it all worthwhile. How's the ME doing, by the way?"

"Good. Real good. He would have been doing a lot more if you'd given me a few more minutes."

"No time," Tanya said matter-of-factly. "We have to come up with a plan."

"What plan? There's no plan."

"Okay then. We'll just have to lie. I'll tell the chef you drink—"

"I'll tell him you drove me to it. Who wouldn't believe that? On top of everything we wouldn't be lying."

"Perhaps I should point out the error of your thinking in casting aspersions upon my character, dear heart."

"What character, Tanya? You have no character." The words came out without so much as a pause, and Beluga was immediately filled with regret.

Tanya's lips formed a horrified "o." She sat still as stone, then promptly went into an overdrive of action that led to disrupting piles of magazines on side tables, and combing through knick-knacks on shelves.

"Look, I'm really—what on earth are you doing?"

"What do you care?"

"I care."

"No you don't. But since you asked," she said, popping open a drawer to the secretary's desk, "I'm trying to find a tissue for the tears I'm barely holding back." She produced a box, pulled out one tissue after another like gunfire and blew her nose with a sound akin to a flock of geese taking flight.

"Feel better?"

"No. And, in case you were wondering, I hate you."

"Ah-ha! You do feel better. Good."

"I don't feel better and you can't make me."

Anger was an emotion Tanya relished, especially under stress, and clearly she wasn't going to let it go very easily this time. Beluga could do only so much. The rest became a question of time.

"Look, Tanya, you took me away from my happy daydream, and I'm a little cranky, what with the pickle we're in. Give me a minute to adjust to this world again. In the meantime, please accept my apology for what I said. It was uncalled for, unfair, and I'm sorry."

"That, my dear, is so true. You are sorry."

Beluga sighed. So that was the way it was going to be today. She had a minute to get over things, Tanya would take what seemed a lifetime. Not to mention a pound of flesh while she was at it. Great.

Tanya sat at the secretary's desk and rifled distractedly through the stacks of papers. "You are a sorry person. Sorry, sorry, sorry. And your little cat, too."

Paw stilled at chin level, Planchette stopped washing his face and looked at her.

"She's in a mood, Planchette. Ignore her."

He looked from one woman to the other, paused, then continued his ablutions.

"You've even got a cat questioning my character," Tanya wailed. She stood then, mustered up full indignation, and spoke through clenched teeth. "I don't need to take this anymore." With one solid sweep of her arm a pile of fat file folders slid almost soundlessly from the desk, to land in a cluttered, disjointed heap on the indoor-outdoor carpet.

Planchette skittered out of the way just as the papers landed. One small leap took him behind a display of decorative silk ficus trees next to the chef's office door.

Beluga was more straightforward. After jumping to her feet, she crossed the room with a conservation of steps, pointed an accusing finger at Tanya, spluttered a series of guttural sounds, then fell to her knees to gather the mess.

"Now who's got no character?" Tanya said in an imperious tone.

Beluga looked up at her friend. "Do you ever listen to yourself?"

"Not if I can help it."

"Perhaps that's best."

"Yes," Tanya said, her tone softening. "I suppose it is. And you know what?"

"I can hardly wait to hear."

"I think I feel better."

"Great."

"Now I only hate you a little bit."

"Fabulous."

"So your apology is accepted."

"Fine. Help me pick up these papers. And do it

quick. Ned Niblett will be summoning us at any moment, and I don't want to explain this insult on top of all the injury."

Tanya lowered herself to the papers to start collating. "Good for you. It's about time you finally owned up."

"Owned up? To what?" Beluga gathered a series of papers, then stopped when one of particular interest caught her eye.

"Owned up to the fact you insulted me. You know. Insult and injury. I've had both in one day, what with the fall and the nasty character comment."

"You fell on me." She scanned the paper, then reached for the next one. "Whatever."

"Are you listening to me?"

Then there was another page. All part of a single personnel file. Interesting. If she played her cards right, and she always did—well, most of the time she did— this information might come in mighty handy. Mighty handy indeed—

"Ahem."

Her response was instinct really; born of the early years when snooping and getting caught in the act went hand in hand. So when Ned Niblett appeared without benefit of any sound whatsoever until his "ah-hem," Beluga's response was pure instinct. Primal. She thrust her paper-filled hand behind her back, offered him a guilty look and a dry swallow, then spoke with a quaver in her voice. "I didn't do anything."

"That so?" he asked, looking over the top of his glasses. "Then who did?"

Beluga was not proud of herself with the next comment, but she rationalized it was the truth, and that at least was something. "She did."

The chef's unblinking gaze fell upon Tanya, who withered like a wax flower thrust into a flame. "Is this true?"

"I...uh...I...well..."

"You don't say."

"I'm trying to, for heaven's sake," she said, a defensive edge to her voice. "Give me a sec."

Their conversation proved time enough for a distraction. Beluga rose, tossed the handful of papers behind the silk trees, and Planchette raked them under himself before the chef had a chance to turn his sleep-deprived and lonely evil eye back to her.

And then Beluga saw something else. There. Sitting as pretty as you please on a chair just inside the chef's office. It had no doubt been dropped there when he heard the disturbance in the waiting room and came to investigate.

"Okay. I think I'm ready now." Tanya continued as best she could, but her excuse came out flat like a practiced recitation. "No. Of course I didn't do it. Why would anyone do a thing like this? We were waiting for you and suddenly, just like that, the papers were everywhere." She looked at the chef to see if he was buying it, opened her eyes wide in what Beluga knew as the "attempted doe look," and finished her story. "It was really quite an astounding thing to see."

"You saw it happen?"

"Sure. You could even say I was close enough that I felt a part of it."

"So you're saying," he looked back and forth between the women, "that this mess is the result of a supernatural event?"

"Well," Tanya said, sweeping her foot in front of her like an innocent little girl buying time to dream up the next scene of her story, "I'm...I...well..." The attempted doe look turned to one caught in headlights at night. She pointed a lethal talon-like fingernail at Beluga. "She drinks."

Beluga glared at Tanya. "Thanks so much. But if you don't mind, I'll do the talking now."

"And I drove her to it," Tanya blurted. She squirmed, grimaced, then blinked at a rapid clip as if a sudden dust storm was aimed solely at her face. "That didn't come out right."

"My turn to talk now." She raised her hand to stop Tanya's protest. "Funny you should bring up the supernatural question."

Ned Niblett turned to Beluga. "How so?"

"We saw it, him, tonight. Twice. In the flesh, as it were."

"You didn't see anything." His face turned rigid. "Because there's nothing to see."

"Oh, but we did."

Tanya piped up then. "We sure did. Both of us. He was going after Planchette, so we chased them. Down the stairs, through the lobby, and into the kitchen. To be more exact, Beluga and Planchette chased him into the kitchen. I had other duties by that time."

"Tanya," Beluga warned. "Don't."

"I was the lookout."

"Planchette?" the chef asked. "I don't remember any student named Planchette."

"He's not a student." Tanya rolled her eyes.

"*Tanya.*"

"He's Beluga's cat."

Time stopped for an eternity, or maybe only a fraction of a second that felt like an eternity, until Ned Niblett swept his glasses off his nose in one clean motion. He swiveled around, seemed to suddenly grow in size to about that of a food distributor supply truck, and loomed over Beluga.

Leaning so far back that a gold medal in Olympic gymnastics was no longer far-fetched, she stared as the chef's face turned blood-red from rope-sized veins that popped out on his neck. He was gonna blow if—

"You brought *a cat* into my kitchen?" he roared.

She cringed at the sound and knew she'd never hear high frequencies again. A nervous smile played across her lips. "Kind of."

Chapter 12

Beluga groaned. "Well, that didn't go well."

She rose from her haunches to dip a large scrubbing brush into the bucket. Wincing at the strong chemical smell, she crinkled her nose, and deposited more liquid onto the tile floor in front of her to work out a particularly recalcitrant food stain. Already her back ached, and she knew that cleaning the kitchen floor from this cat's eye view couldn't be doing her injured knee one bit of good.

"Tell me about it." Tanya worked out of another bucket a few steps away.

"You had to mention Planchette. You had to tell the chef Planchette was a cat."

"He is a cat. What? I should tell him he's the food and beverage manager?"

"You didn't need to tell him anything. I told you I'd do all the talking. Why didn't you let me do the talking?"

"Look. I'm sorry. What more do you want me to do?"

"You could clean out the grease trap. It's next on the list."

"No can do. That's one solid piece of nastiness. And you don't even want to know what kind of wildlife can grow in there."

"I'll bet Chef Pernod knows."

"That she does. And thanks to her, so do I. So trust me when I say after seeing that trap I may never eat fried food again."

"I guess you haven't seen what's fallen behind the meat slicer then."

Tanya wagged her scrubbing brush at Beluga. "Do you want to give me nightmares? Is that what you want? 'Cause if that's what you want, then you've got it. This whole place is a nightmare, and I wouldn't be here in the first place if not for you."

"No one twisted your arm to come here. Besides, if not here you'd be paying good money to pretend you're some kind of deranged soap on an elastic rope."

"It's called bungee-jumping, and it beats the hell out of cleaning a commercial kitchen because the chef doesn't believe in ghosts."

"Ladies, ladies." Bob Blanchard, security guard, touched a finger to his lips to quiet them. "I'm begging you. The other cooking students will be here shortly and there's a lot left to do." He leaned back in his chair and tapped his watch. "Time is ticking."

Tanya snorted. "It would go a lot faster if you helped."

"Sorry, ma'am. This is your punishment. Mine is coming when I get home and the wife hands me a list of errands to do."

"You've got a wife? Figures. I can't get a break around here. Hey! You're not doing anything now."

"I've got plenty of things to keep me occupied," Bob said, holding up a magazine.

"That's it? That's your only excuse for not helping us out?" Tanya pitched her brush into the gray wash water. "Well, maybe I'll use the same excuse. Too many other things to keep me occupied. What do you think about that?"

He looked at her over the top of his magazine. "Not much."

"So I quit. And nothing you can say or do will change my mind."

"I've got a gun."

"Oh."

"No need for violence, Bob." Beluga turned to Tanya. "At least not until I give you the signal to fire. Then, by all means, fire at will."

"Are you starting with me again?" Tanya reached into the murky depths for her scrubbing brush and waved it around. "Because you are working my last nerve, and I can't be responsible for what happens when it goes."

Beluga crawled over to Tanya, glanced at the security guard who was once again immersed in his reading, then motioned they should start work on the floors again.

Scritch, scritch, scritch, went the brushes on the tile. The sound was enough to cover their whispers.

"I don't know if Ned Niblett believes in ghosts or not."

"Trust me, I know," Tanya said. "He doesn't."

Scritch.

"But I'll tell you this, Tanya. He believes in cluricauns. And after all this, so do I. Certainly Planchette does. And you, too, for that matter."

"How can I believe in something when I have no idea what you're talking about?"

Bob Blanchard shifted in his chair.

"Scrub," Beluga ordered.

They did.

A minute passed. Two.

Beluga sidled closer to Tanya. "The little man, the one we saw chasing Planchette, the one drinking all the liquor?"

"Yeah."

"There's no doubt in my mind. He's a cluricaun."

Tanya sat back on her knees and stretched out her back. "Well, that's about as clear as mud. What's a cluricaun?"

"If memory serves...he's a cousin of the leprechaun. The black sheep of the family by virtue of his antics."

"That includes drinking and harassing cats?"

"Bingo!"

"*Apo ti apotelite afto to piato*? What does this dish consist of?"

"Maybe more than we want on our plates right now. By the way, Bob's a security guard at a cooking school. He doesn't carry a gun."

Tanya froze. "Why that—"

"Never mind. It's not important. What's important is that Ned Niblett may not believe in ghosts, but he sure can't deny there's a cluricaun stuck to him like glue."

"I thought only poltergeists did that."

"Me, too," Beluga conceded. "But let's review. Where there's Ned Niblett, there's this cluricaun. Stranger things have happened."

"Yeah. And all of them around you. How did you know the little man was a cluricaun by the way?"

"I have a mind and a memory like a steel trap."

"Come on. You may have a wealth of knowledge

in some of the most obscure topics anyone could dream of, particularly when it comes to the realm of metaphysics, but your memory is far from a…whatever you said before."

"He was close enough to a leprechaun. That much I know, although I've never seen one up close and that personal. But he's a little off the profile of a true leprechaun."

"And…"

"And the book I saw on a chair just inside the chef's office cleared up the matter rather clearly."

"There was a book?"

"There's a book for just about everything, Tanya. You just have to know where to find them."

"Or have a need to find them. So, Ned Niblett. A book. Cluricaun. Glue. Does that pretty well sum things up?"

"There's just one flaw in that theory."

"Only one?"

"Now's not the time for snippiness, Tanya." She cocked her head toward the large garbage can filled with liquor bottles. "When it comes to spirits of the alcohol variety, the cluricaun seemed to be working alone. That makes me wonder if his supernatural abilities could be up to more than relatively harmless antics."

"Like murder?"

"Bingo again. But why?"

Tanya moaned. "There's always another question. And now I have one of my own. Why is everything so difficult with you?"

"Would you have it any other way?" Beluga nudged her, then nudged her again until she smiled.

"No. I guess not."

"Unless Ned Niblett is the murderer and the cluricaun just happened to be a good front."

"See?" Tanya's lips turned into a scowl. "Difficult."

"The chef has the access. He has the ability and knowledge. It's just the motive angle that's a little murky."

"Always difficult."

"But never boring." Beluga glanced at the window to the dining room. "Here come the students. This may be our excuse to wrap things up." She leaned in close to Tanya and whispered, "You know what to do."

The door to the kitchen swung open, and as expected, Katie Cliff was the first one in, and chattering to no one in particular.

"Sauces today. And how fun is that going to be. Fun, fun, fun. In fact, if I didn't have a middle name already, I'd make sure my middle name was fun 'cause that's how I feel." She turned the corner and stopped as if she slammed face first into a wall. "What is that smell? Is that alcohol?"

Tony came in right behind her. Already on task for the day, he'd gotten clear across the kitchen before the sound of his steel-toed shoes came to an abrupt halt. "Yup. Liquor. And a lot of it. All mixed together."

Within minutes the kitchen filled with chef students. Some were more worse for the wear after last night's party than others, but all took the time to congregate around Beluga and Tanya in blatant curiosity.

"You didn't get to cook something special, did you?" asked Katie. "'Cause if you did that's not fair, and I'll have to tell someone."

"Does it look like we're cooking?" snarled Tanya. "Because if it does, you can just drop your bony ass right here on the floor and whip up something."

Beluga jumped in before a full-blown argument developed. "Tanya, Katie, please."

Tanya dropped the brush into the water, stood, and kicked the bucket through the crowd while mumbling, "I don't know what it is about kitchens and cooking, but it just gets to me. All of it. Just gets to me. And then some bony ass student without the sense of a pinecone goes and says something stupid, and..." She lumbered around the corner with the bucket and an *I dare you* glare to Bob Blanchard, then disappeared.

"Somebody is not having fun today." Katie sighed, then smiled broadly. "But that doesn't mean the rest of us can't, right?" On the spot, she proclaimed herself school monitor and started counting off students via a checkmark in the air. And all the while she never stopped talking. "Today is a good day. Check. A special day. Check. A day of sauces for some of us, and more delicious breads for you in the baking—" She stopped then, and looked about the kitchen and the dispersing students who ignored her to pursue more immediate tasks. "Something's wrong."

"More than you can ever imagine, dear," Beluga said while trying to hoist herself up.

"Need some help?"

Beluga looked up and saw Tony. Sweet, knight-in-shining-armor Tony. Always ready and available when she needed him. "Yea, good sir. A hand would be most welcome now."

"Whatever you say." He pulled, she rocked in

place and stayed.

"Bum knee."

"Yeah. It looks kinda swollen. Maybe you shouldn't be on it."

"I'm not on it now, more's the pity. No telling what's going to happen when I do finally get up."

"Something's wrong," Katie Cliff announced again.

Tony tried pulling Beluga again to no avail, and shouted for assistance. A modest core of caring students came to the rescue, wrangled Beluga up, and stood her on a hand truck thoughtfully produced by Bob Blanchard. She would have preferred a travel method other than the film-depicted one used to transport a charming, smart, sociopath who liked to eat people, but at this point she would take what she could get.

Bob held his breath, tipped the hand truck ever so slightly back, and with Tony's assistance wheeled Beluga toward the door to the dining room.

"Isn't anybody listening to me?" Katie asked. "*Stop it. Stop it, all of you.*"

The clinking of nested baking pans being separated stopped. Rolling carts bearing mixers and food processors stilled. Measuring cups filled with assorted ingredients came to rest on steel tables, while utensils were caught mid-use, but silenced.

"Where's Jeanette?" Katie asked simply.

Tony whispered into Beluga's ear. "Jackleg."

"Yes. I'm familiar with that moniker."

A series of shrugs, and who cares punctuated the silence, followed by one anonymous, "Maybe she's sleeping it off."

"Okay," Katie said. "Just checking. It's good to

know who's here and who isn't, right? It separates the real chefs from the hopefuls, huh? Everybody, back to work."

A lone anonymous middle-finger salute appeared from between two reach-in refrigerators.

Katie's eyes widened at the act, but she offered no response.

At last, here was an action that actually rendered the annoying Katie wordless, however briefly. Good to know, and something that might come in handy one day.

Beluga was wheeled into the dining room. The trio arrived at the swinging doors and exited without Tony who had returned to the kitchen to start his *mise* for the day. Bob Blanchard, the perpetual gentleman guard, broke into a sweat, but didn't stop pushing his cargo.

"Over there by the cocktail and espresso bar will be just fine, thank you. Gives me a place to lean against."

"You got it." He did as he was told, righted the hand truck, and stepped back to catch his breath while offering a sympathetic mandate. "Now don't move a muscle."

"You can count on it, Mr. Blanchard."

"The chef said you were to finish up the cleaning and then get to work on cooking, but I reckon he wasn't expecting an injury such as this."

"I reckon not."

"So I gotta go find out what he wants me to do next." He reluctantly backed up a couple of steps.

"You do that."

"Not a muscle," he said, clearly in an attempt at admonition. Instead his words seemed almost welcoming.

"Not a single one." Her voice softened at his manner and her upcoming guilt.

"Okay, then." He paused as if refereeing an argument in his head, declared a winner, then sauntered to chef's office.

While grudgingly admitting to herself she was splitting semantic hairs, she didn't move a single muscle as promised; rather she moved whole groupings of them. Stepping off the hand truck, she winced at the pain in her knee that was annoying, but far from debilitating, and leaned over the bar. "Come out, come out wherever you are."

Sleepy green eyes in a feline face topped by pyramidal ears emerged over the edge of the counter.

"There you are my handsome boy. I trust you got some welcome rest."

Planchette yawned deep and long.

"Wish I could say the same for myself, but as usual, there's no rest for the weary. Or those in deep trouble."

She limped out of the dining room, back through the lobby, and headed up the stairwell to the dorm room she shared with Tanya. Planchette followed close on her heels while scanning their surroundings.

"That's right, boy. Sing out if you see any cluricauns, chefs, or security guards. We've little time to spare if I'm going to change out of these nasty clothes and kick this investigation up a notch."

One flight after another, then another, Beluga arrived at her floor breathless and holding her sides as if her internal organs were about to spill out, or explode. Organ explosion as a diversion was a little something she'd keep in mind so she'd be ready should the need arise. She stopped, saw it and almost appreciated such a dramatic display.

Planchette came up to stand next to her and stared as well.

The door to her dorm room was wide open.

And there, just outside the door was a lone shoe.

Was someone waiting for her? Because if they were, she was far from the kind of mood needed to graciously welcome visitors.

The hair on her neck and arms suddenly jumped to attention. A chill crept down her spine.

No visitors here, she knew. Not this time. But no doubt about it, there was something definitely wrong. What was it that waited for her in the room?

A supernatural manifestation?

No.

Not supernatural this time. It was something all too real.

Real, but fleeting. A remnant. A piece.

She shook her head as if to clear the cloudiness in her mind's eye; to settle things into a picture she could understand. But there wasn't enough information yet. Not quite enough to get more than an uneasy feeling and a growing sense of dread.

A door at the other end of the hallway slammed open with a solid thud into the wall. Tanya lunged out, gulped for air, then used the wall to keep herself upright while she walked toward their room.

"Be careful," Beluga warned in a stage whisper.

Tanya offered a weak wave, crossed the hall to the bed frames left outside the dorm room for the party, and collapsed onto a set of metal springs that instantly dropped her to within inches of the floor. "The Empire

State Building should have so many steps. What? They can't put in an elevator with what they charge? This is a horrible place."

Beluga walked to the edge of the door, just shy of looking in. "Do you feel it?"

"Screams from every muscle in my body? Yeah. And then some."

"Rather, do you feel the lack of something? You know, something, or someone here one minute and gone the next?"

"Uh-oh. You're getting that look again."

"What look?"

"The look you get when something's coming to you. I don't like that look. It means something bad is about to happen."

Beluga took a deep breath, stepped into the doorway, and scanned the room. "It can also mean something bad has already happened."

Tanya wrestled with the bed frame to free herself, but to no avail. "What? What's happened? Damn it. Help me out of here so I can see, too."

"Maybe it's best if you stay there. I don't want you to corrupt the crime scene."

Tanya pushed against the sides of the bed frame, twisted, turned, and winced as the springs gripped tighter than ever. "If this thing were a man he would have had to buy me dinner." She squirmed even more, then sank lower until her rump rested solidly on the floor. "It's like I've been consumed by quicksand." She looked up from her trap then. "Did you say *crime scene*?"

"I'm afraid so, Tanya. I'm afraid so."

Chapter 13

From: Office of Admissions
To: All Culinary Students

Dear All Students:
You have been accepted into the culinary arts program for the summer quarter. Attendance at an interrogation session is required, so we have taken the liberty of scheduling you for tonight's session. If this time is not convenient for you, please notify the police as soon as possible so that an alternate time can be arranged. Space permitting.

Please note, you have been accepted into a specialized program based on the rich heritage of established culinary principles. If you expect to refine your abilities in preparing the typical North Georgia "Cake with Hidden Hacksaw," or any variation on jail cuisine, you may need to reconsider your acceptance.

We look forward to seeing you at tonight's interrogation session, and know that your culinary experience will be a rewarding one.

Sincerely,
Petula Brock
Admissions

****

Beluga Stein's Diary
No "bon appétit" or "happy cooking" will be

uttered today, the way things are shaping up. Tanya mumbled something in Greek about train stations and locker keys, but right now no one seems to find particular interest in European transportation or storage issues.

Upon finding the note there was nothing for it but that I should bring it to the attention of Ned Niblett and Bob Blanchard. They in turn discovered their hands would be tied, literally handcuffed as it were, if they overlooked mentioning this find to the local authorities. So that's what they did.

After the recent death of a well-liked chef, the powers-that-be wasted no time arriving at the school en masse to see for themselves what exactly was being cooked up. Alas, the verdict rendered revealed the note was not a fabrication. It had all the ingredients to put the school in the stew and the students in a pickle.

I find word play a much needed diversion when I'm under stress.

Others have their own methods of dealing with anxiety. Planchette grooms himself to a near sterile and hairless state—which is an option I prefer not to take, even if I knew how—and Tanya interferes with evidence and information gathering by trolling for bachelors among the steady stream of new male arrivals. If not for her attempt to master another language, efforts to corral unsuspecting incoming law enforcement for Tanya's own lecherous purposes might be even more laser-focused and unblinking than usual. No one can unsee that.

But I digress since Tanya couldn't practice discretion if it bit her in the... anywhere. And, btw, I must digress again since a surge of electricity shot up my spine to reside in my neck when putting together the words "Tanya," "lecherous," and "bite" all in one thought. She would love the precision and, well, accuracy of the connected words. Would that I could, however, unthink the disturbing image.

Anyhoo, the note found in our shared dorm room was not a fabrication being that it was a real note, specifically a confession. But the signature at the bottom, "Jeannete Regena Mason," was a bit off the mark considering the supposed note writer would know how to spell her own name correctly. Besides, the handwriting was all wrong, too, as witnessed by Jackleg's notes found in a book of collected recipes and observations.

The argument was raised about Jackleg's questionable lucidity after a night of consuming large quantities of Dromedary Spit.

P.S. Try explaining that to the authorities. So, perhaps a case could be made for the misspelling and handwriting problems. Perhaps. What couldn't be explained was why she suddenly felt compelled to write a note confessing to the murder of Chef John Doe. I mean, why would she do that? What connection did they have to create a motive for such a deed? Well... aside from the fact Jackleg said she hated Chef Doe? At least, sometimes she disliked him.

And then there was that other pesky matter of her immediate and surprising vast knowledge of cocktail garnish. More extensive knowledge of vegetation couldn't be too far behind. Furthermore, one must ask, could the use of Lily of the Valley be in Jackleg's repertoire, too?

Not that she was talking.

Did I mention she was unavailable for questioning on these topics? Not passed out where we left her, mind you, she simply wasn't there at all. In fact, after a lockdown and search of the entire facility Jackleg was nowhere to be found. The only thing left of hers was a size 8 1/2 shoe that showed a worn heel, (and bad taste according to Tanya's forensic opinion), her initials on the inside, and a double scuff mark across the floor.

Now I don't pretend to know all the ins and outs of police investigation techniques, but it seemed pretty clear to me she was dragged to the door and lost a shoe in the process. And it seemed highly unlikely in that brief interim of drag-pause-stop-lose-shoe that she would have sobered up enough to suddenly muster the capability of walking out the building on her own steam. Unnoticed to boot.

Murder? It was possible.

A confession written out of guilt? Maybe.

A disappearing act by dragging herself out the door so that only her heels made contact with the floor? No way.

And why, I must ask, would anyone feel the need to put their initials in a shoe? Was there some kind of footwear crime no one has taken the time to make me aware of?

Something was fishy. Really fishy. And it was not sushi grade.

****

Beluga tucked her diary and pen into her large handbag, looked at her watch, then at Petula Brock, Director of Admissions.

"Don't even think about it," the surly and humorless woman said. "I was told to keep an eye on you and that is what I aim to do."

"But—"

"—As if there wasn't enough madness in this place already. Paperwork up to my ears, the coffee machine on the fritz again, and not a pastry in sight thanks to the shut down in the baking class."

"Again—"

"Didn't even bring my lunch because we were told the students were making a meal today. Not that I like all that fancy-schmancy stuff half the time, but it works for the old pocketbook and keeps the rumbling in my bowels quiet. Maybe I can talk someone into a little boiled chicken or some fried luncheon meat. I mean, a girl's gotta eat, doesn't she?

"Maybe—"

Petula Brock leaned across the desk to Beluga. "I have a…what's it called? A delicate constituency."

"Could you mean 'constitution?'"

"Whatever. All I know is one false move, and it could blow at any time."

Planchette's ears folded back. The tip of his tail twitched, yet his gaze remained fixed on Petula Brock.

Beluga scooted her chair back. "Do alert me ahead of time should you feel your, er, *constituency* prepare to blow. We'd like to be out of the path of the storm."

"Wish I could. I just never know when it's gonna happen. A pastry about now would help though. You know, kinda plug things up and all."

"Try that desk over there," Beluga said, hoping she was right.

Bread product intuition could be a dicey thing.

The admissions director swiveled in her chair for a look across the office. "Food? Claire's desk?"

"Third drawer down on the right."

"But she's on a diet."

Beluga shrugged. Wasn't everybody?

"Maybe I'll just take a little look-see being as how she snoops through my desk all the time when I'm not here." She rose from her chair and moved stealth-like across the room. Or as stealth-like as she could with her squeaking shoes, clumping gait, rumbling bowels, and loud accusations.

It was the break Beluga and Planchette had been waiting for.

"Always snooping. Trying to find proof I'm having a thing with her husband, that's what she's doing. And she thinks I don't know." Petula Brock laughed bitterly, then squeaked, clumped, rumbled, and accused over another few steps. "Of course I know. I know everything she does. And some things she doesn't. At least according to her husband."

Beluga didn't wait to see if her bakery prediction had been correct. There was no time. Before the police arrived she had made a quick call to Doc to set the arrangements. Now all she had to do was meet him at the appointed time and at the appointed place.

"Planchette," she whispered, then cocked her head toward a door that led outside.

Planchette stared at the admissions director for another beat, then sauntered toward the door.

"Remember, don't give anyone a clear shot when we get out there. Serpentine, boy. Serpentine." Beluga knocked the door open with her hip, then loped in small half-circles to one side of the woods, then the other, back and forth just like she had seen in movies when people escaped gunfire. There was no gunfire here, but better safe than sorry.

She serpentined through the woods that ran along one side of the school. Planchette kicked up his pace into a lope, but stayed true without the slightest nod to a serpentine. No wasted energy with that one, and not even the slightest hint of panting. She snorted with what breath she had left as the two of them emerged by a little used parking lot, just in time for Doc to screech to a stop in a very exotic car.

"I said inconspicuous."

"It is inconspicuous."

Beluga eyed the car. "It's clearly expensive. It's got no roof and it's eye-popping red."

"It is anything but inconspicuous."

"It's inconspicuous in that most people around here have never seen a beauty like this."

"Should I have used other words like modest, or unobtrusive, or, say, low-key, to get the point across that it's best we aren't noticed? I'm not supposed to leave the school. I could get into a lot of trouble."

"Better to look good than to feel good," he said, gunning the engine to a far more screaming pitch than was necessary.

"Yeah. No one will notice me in this car. It might as well have 'arrest me' written all over the side panel the way neither of us will be noticed."

"Trust me. They may notice the car. It'll never occur to anyone you're in it."

"Swell."

"Get in."

Planchette jumped into Doc's lap.

Beluga reached for the tiny handle on the tiny half-door.

"No, no. Jump over it. Quicker. And infinitely more fun."

"Jump? You've got to be kidding."

Petula Brock unexpectedly burst through the woods, hollering, and waving one hand madly while the other clutched an overly large muffin.

"I'll jump if you swear to me this thing can move."

Doc nodded. "It's been successful at Sebring. And Le Mans. North Georgia doesn't have a prayer."

"Here goes nothing." Beluga jumped toward the door, caught her shin on the edge, and fell partway into the car. "Go, go, go, *go*."

"Your legs aren't in."

"They're connected to the part that is in. Will you just go?"

"There's not a lot of throttle, but I'll do the best I can." Doc let out the clutch and they moved suddenly and abruptly as if shot out of a cannon when something smacked against the windshield. "What the hell was that?"

Beluga pulled in her legs, squirmed to an upright position and stared at the blob that seemed glued to the glass. "I'm guessing lemon-poppy seed."

"What?"

"A breakfast bread product. Or, in this case, an ammo muffin."

"Some kind of company you keep, huh?"

"Don't start on me, Doc. And besides, what does it say about your company?"

They hit a speed bump on their way out of the parking lot that launched Planchette out of the car.

Without a glance Doc reached into the air to capture the cat like a fly ball, and brought Planchette back to the safety of his lap. "Independent, double wishbones, coil springs front suspension." He slid a pair of sunglasses over his eyes, smiled broadly, and pulled out into the limited access four-lane. "It doesn't get better than this."

"Or more noticeable. And, to reiterate by the way, I specifically used the word 'inconspicuous.'"

"And I specifically heard 'quick getaway.'"

"At least you're not naked."

"That could change in a blink of an eye."

"Please. Not in front of my eyes."

He smiled again and picked up the speed by alternately pushing the gas and clutch pedals in a rapid and precise pattern that brought Beluga's head forward, backward, and bouncing side to side all at an equal clip. At this rate she'd be a dashboard head-nodding dog ornament in no time, but without the perpetual happy face.

They reached cruising speed at some g-force, the number of which Beluga could only speculate. It wouldn't surprise her to see the ocean any minute. Landfall someplace in Europe would undoubtedly arrive shortly after that.

Fortunately, traffic was light today. Besides, the few cars that were on the road would barely notice this car passing them save for an undecipherable blur and a sound that rattled their doors some minutes later.

She gathered her thoughts, looked ahead and behind, then spoke hesitantly for fear of his answer to her statement. "We're going the wrong way."

"Okay," he said simply.

There was nothing at first, so she allowed herself the luxury to initiate a deep breath. Then there was something. Something big and potentially life-threatening, she knew. But then Doc wouldn't have it any other way. The breath she had hoped to complete resisted, then stuck in her throat like the last jelly bean stuck to the bottom of a glass container. Both purchased decades ago.

The car groaned with a sudden drop in momentum, although far, far short of a full stop. A twist of the steering wheel fishtailed the back of the car and spewed a blue-gray cloud that billowed into a mushroom shape from under the back wheels. They plummeted into the dipped, grassy median.

In an explosion of power and hurled clods of dirt, they emerged on the other side of the median to skid onto the asphalt where it was doubtful if the tires would hold. The tires held. In the process, the heated rubber left a permanent visual history of the moment. Then, like the magic of now you see it, now you don't, they were off in the direction from whence they came. Planchette had grabbed on to anything with all four sets of claws in a splayed position that would make even a cartoon character jealous.

Doc shouted over the roar of the engine, "Is this the way? 'Cause if it's not I'll be glad to turn her around again."

"*No*," she wheezed with the minimum breath left in her lungs to sustain life.

"O-kaay," he said with mock innocence.

The frequent and rapid sequence of hand and foot, hand and foot, started the down-shifting anew.

She gasped deeply enough to shout over the thunder of the engine, "I mean, no, don't turn around again. This is the way we want to go."

Disappointment flickered across his face. "Are you sure? Won't take but a second."

"I can't tell you how sure I am."

"Really sure? Wouldn't want to waste any time or anything."

"I think this car can alter time. It certainly took years off my life."

"Funny," he said. "It makes me feel a lot younger."

Beluga dug deep into her massive pocketbook to retrieve the file she lifted from Ned Niblett's office. Hurricane force winds formed jetties in and around the car and threatened to snatch the papers out of her hand and set them free.

"Where to?" Doc asked.

"That's what I'm trying to find out. But this is like trying to do surgery in a tempest. No one's happy with the results."

"Okay," he said.

She shored up for what could be another of Doc's daredevil maneuvers, but was cheered to see he was simply coming to a stop. Not a gradual stop, but an ultimate and bold cessation of movement by the car as it tore through the wildflowers planted on the shoulder of the road. Her body, however, had yet to get the halt message. She was lifted out of the seat and thrown forward, fearing the distinct possibility of becoming intimate with the long curves of the hood, followed by a wildlife view of the grill, and ending with Department of Transportation-planted poppies lodged in her teeth.

Better to look good than to feel good.

Fortunately she could do both since she popped back into the low, snug seat without injury and barely a whimper.

"Are we having fun yet?"

"Loads." She rifled through the papers in the file.

"Now if this isn't the right direction—"

"I'll make it the right direction."

"Spoilsport."

"Sticks and stones…" She pulled out a page, ran a finger down the print, and tapped. "Here it is."

"Our destination?"

"Yup. And blessed be most things edible, we are indeed faced in the correct direction. Just a few miles straight ahead, then make a right on…Booger-Holler Way."

"You made that up."

"I'm telling you. It's true. And then a left on Holler Road proper and another left on All The Trout You Can Eat Boulevard."

"Where is the sense of propriety? Of watching out for the future?" Doc smacked the steering wheel. "Did any of these people give a second's thought when they named the locations of their domains?"

"A second. Two at most."

Something slammed against the windshield. Planchette loosened his four-point cartoon character death grip and dove deeper between the passenger floorboard and the glove compartment.

"What the hell is it this time?"

Beluga squinted, reached around the edge of the windshield, and dropped a small sample of the ammo into her mouth. "Banana-nut. Did you really have to stop in front of the school? I mean, of all places, we had to stop almost where we began?"

Doc threw the car into gear, propelling them out of the wildflowers and onto the road in a tornado-type display of green, red, and occasional purple vegetation. "How many muffin grenades does this woman have?"

"Claire's on a diet," she said as if this would clear everything up. "There's no telling how vast the arsenal might be. But you should probably be afraid."

"I'll make a note of it."

"A few miles, then Booger, Holler, and Trout."

"And then?"

"And then we see what Chef Doe's cabin has to offer this investigation."

"The Lily of the Valley case?"

"The very same."

Doc nodded and pressed the gas pedal for a little extra speed. "Now you're talking."

"Speaking of talking, let me use your phone for a minute."

"How do you know I have one?" He reached into his pocket and gave it to her.

"Everyone besides me has one. Toddlers even have them now from what I hear. They ring in when it's time for a diaper change. How do you work this thing?"

Doc supplied a quick lesson punctuated by moments of life-changing fear when they drifted off the road to pick up additional flora. Beluga's anxiety dropped to a consistent dread when she finally heard ringing.

"Darwin! So good to hear your voice. Trust me when I say it may be the last time, so let's make it count." Beluga gestured Doc for the turn, but they overshot it. "That was Booger Holler Way. Go back."

"Okay."

"Hold on, Darwin," she said into the phone. "I'll be with you in a sec—"

Doc didn't bother with the median this time. With a scream of gears and a cloud of smoke that enveloped them, they spun around three-quarters of a circle and gravel flew into the intersection while Doc fought the shoulder to put the car onto the new road.

"Yes, Darwin. You heard right. Booger Holler Way. And," she said for the benefit of Doc, "a left on Holler Road. You drive past this turn and I'll kill you with a tire iron and leather cleaner. What's that, Darwin? Long story that's best told in a bar, preferably one that doesn't move. Hold on again. We're coming up on Holler Road. Left. Left. *Left.*"

The turn was uneventful for the most part, save for a woman who would probably never line dry her laundry again.

"Left on All The Trout You Can Eat Boulevard and we're home free. Darwin, I'm calling about John Doe. Got any news? Yes, I know it's early and you've scarcely had a chance. Yes, I know you're trying to squeeze in medical school in your spare time. And yes, I remember your concern about body parts and slings. Hold on again. I'm going to put you and the phone in my pocket since we're coming up on the next road at the speed of sound. Don't hang up whatever you do. Left, Doc. *Left.*"

All The Trout You Can Eat Boulevard provided no trout, no eating establishments, and no kind of thoroughfare that by anyone's stretch of the imagination could be considered a boulevard. It was barely a logging road. Rarely used tire ruts sat on either side of a continuous mound of thriving weeds that battered the underside of the car with a rhythmic *thwacka-thwacka-thwacka*. Alongside the road was a series of scruffy trees that eventually became mature, varied in their genus and species, and offered a canopy of shade that was most welcome.

Doc, who appreciated remoteness perhaps more than most, now seemed disappointed at the snail's pace his sports car had to endure. Beluga was glad for the change and could even begin to feel her face resume a normal, pre-warp speed configuration. It was good to feel her lips again. The ability to blink was a nice bonus, too.

There, just up ahead at the end of the road, was the cabin. Nothing more, nothing less. Plenty of room for one, quaint enough for two deeply in love, and a bloodbath waiting to happen for three or more who dared occupy the modest place at the same time.

"Is this it?" she asked.

"I'm pretty sure." Doc stopped the car in a small clearing and turned off the engine. "The mailbox said 'Doe,' so it seems likely."

"Nothing gets past you."

"Unless I want it to."

"Shall we to the snooping?"

"That's what we're here for." He grabbed Planchette from under the dashboard, jumped with practiced ease over the door, and lowered the cat to the ground.

Planchette immediately shook himself and started grooming.

"Stick with me, boy, and there'll be a scarf and aviator glasses in it for you."

Planchette seemed less than thrilled at the prospect of another ride, with or without fashion accessories, and sauntered off toward a tree for much needed claw sharpening.

"A little help here," Beluga said.

"Jump out."

"Jumping in is one thing, and I don't need to remind you how that went, but jumping out is not within the realm of physical possibility. Mine or Newton's."

"What are you saying?"

"I'm saying open the damn door."

"Okay." He pulled the handle.

Beluga swayed, squirmed, then tumbled out the door onto the ground. Fortunately it was a short fall. "A hand, please."

He applauded half-heartedly.

"Very funny." She rose to her knees and groaned to a stand. "And you call yourself a man of impeccable manners."

"My taste also runs to broad physical humor."

"I'll ignore that statement in all its meanings for now, but know that revenge will be sweet." She patted dirt off her muumuu, glared at him, then turned her attention to the cabin.

A few old flagstones directed them up the short path to the front door. She knocked, just in case, then stepped to one side to look in the window.

"No one's here. Do you think anyone would mind if we, you know, pried the door open?"

"In the interest of science?"

"Sure. Why not?"

Doc turned the knob and walked in.

"How did you do that?"

"A simple flip of the wrist."

"No ice pick or credit card?"

"Some people still feel comfortable leaving their doors unlocked. At least the ones that don't know about you."

Beluga nodded. "Or the ones that don't feel anything at all anymore." She walked in and studied the living arrangement. "Tragic. It's all so tragic and sad. I never get used to the pain of a passing that came too soon or so violently." She picked up a photograph of Chef Doe in full culinary regalia. "Such a handsome man. He has a depth and kindness in his eyes that's so rare now. It hurts me right in the pit of my belly. What's this?" She scanned the other photos gathered on the side table and zeroed in on one. "Jackleg?"

"Who?"

"A student. She supposedly signed a confession to his killing, but no one knows where she is."

Doc checked out the rest of the one room and stepped into the small bath area for a look. "She's disappeared?"

"Just like that." Beluga looked closer at the photograph. "This isn't right. She looks too young. Much younger than she is now. I don't get it."

Doc returned from the bathroom and went to the refrigerator. The floor creaked under his feet.

"Tell me you're not going to make yourself something to eat."

"On the contrary." He opened the refrigerator door. "The man was a chef, right?"

"Right."

"There's nothing obvious I can find anywhere else. So maybe there's something revealing in here. Huh."

"What?"

"Some of it is getting old."

"Food does that, Doc."

"But some of it is new. Brand new." He held up a package of deli meat and pointed at the date.

"Yesterday new. But how…?"

"My thoughts exactly."

"I'm thinking the police would leave a Do Not Cross tape long before they'd leave wrapped cold cuts." She looked around with some concern. "Someone else has been here. Recently."

"To quote those more masterful in summation than I, 'No shit, Sherlock,'"

"That someone might *still* be here."

"Not unless they hiked in. And that seems unlikely."

A chill covered her then. It started on the surface of her skin, then settled deep into bone. She shivered and closed her eyes against the fear of what she might see if she let the picture form in her mind.

"Someone *is* here."

"Not in this room. Or in the bathroom. Certainly not in the refrigerator." He closed the door and stepped back. The floor groaned under his weight.

"No. But close enough. Somewhere…" She paced the room. "Somewhere…" She stopped suddenly, looked out a back window. "Outside then. We have to look. We have to find her."

"Her?"

"Feminine energy. A her. Definitely."

"Lead on then."

The two left and turned the closest corner to the back of the house. There, among neat, clearly identified sections were the vast components of an impressive herb garden. Lovingly maintained, lustily thriving, and stunning in their varied ornamentation, the place was a picture postcard that most gardeners could spend their whole lives working on and still never achieve. John Doe was considered a chef to be emulated, but his herb garden placed him solidly in the ranks of stardom.

"Breathtaking," Doc said. "Grand in the full sense of the word. I am positively awestruck."

"No. Not here. She's not here." Beluga turned in one direction, then another. Nothing firm came to her except a growing anxiety and sense of dread. A knot settled in her stomach, grew to painful proportions. "Planchette. I need your help. Planchette?"

Her familiar was nowhere to be found.

"Planchette?"

And then she heard him. Off in the distance. But there was another sound as well. Something just as plaintive, and yet urgent.

In the distance. There? No.

Over there? Yes.

She ambled past the herb garden, hiked up her muumuu to skirt the edge of the yard, trotted into a tangle of wildflowers and blackberry bushes. Then broke into as close a full run as she could while thorns prickled her skin, scratched, then drew blood. Never once did she feel pain, or the sticky warmth of blood that formed streaks on her arms and face. There was only pounding in her ears and fear she would be too late. Or was it fear she would be too early?

That didn't matter. What mattered now was that she got there, wherever there was.

Brambles loomed large and painfully dense. She fought back as hard she got from them, and heard her clothes tear and her breath come ragged and shallow.

Yes, this was the right direction, but where specifically did she need to be?

And then she saw it.

Wood. Small. Square. Yet unusually tall. Its once solid walls were now dangerously tenuous. Vents in the tin roof allowed the smoke to escape in its prime, but now long past that point it allowed elements access to the windowless structure and that was never meant to be. Boards that once held the place together now separated and cracked and leaned and screamed with every breath of slight wind that touched them.

The smokehouse had stood for a hundred years.

It wouldn't stand much longer.

Then came the plaintive sounds. One from a cat who had a human nature, the other from someone who was human by nature. Both sounds gave her mental pause and a sense of dread. She plowed through the last few feet of merciless vegetation to yank open the door. It gave with a shriek of hinges being finally and irrevocably torn from grayed wood and fell almost soundlessly into decades' worth of neglected brush.

Planchette didn't turn to meet her gaze, but stared instead at the woman suspended from the weak ceiling beam by rusted wrought iron meat hooks.

Jackleg was alive, relatively uninjured as determined by a cursory look, and weak. More importantly she was pissed and that in itself might have been what kept her among the living. Mustering strength from some source deep inside, she whispered clearly: "Get me the hell out of here." Then she started crying.

"Good. That's good, honey," Beluga said while surveying the damaged building and the hooks through

Jackleg's dirty clothes that kept her suspended well out of reach.

The only thing between her and a potentially lethal drop to Earth was the tight chef jacket she wore backwards so that the buttons were on the back. A straitjacket couldn't have been more effective, and that, Beluga decided, was a strange testament to the profession if not the required attire.

"Just keep talking and we'll do our best to get you out of here. *Doc!*"

He arrived with his own roadmap of angry scratches across his face and arms and took in the scene immediately. "We've got to get her down."

"How? How do we do that? There's not a ladder, or steps, or any way I can see that she got up there in the first place. Tell me how to get her down and I'll do it."

A scream of tearing material filled the small space and dropped Jackleg a few inches on one side. Her crying stopped then. She turned pale. A sheen of sweat appeared on her face and down her arms. Her breathing became shallow.

"She's going into shock. She'll die if we don't do something."

"Talk to me, baby," Beluga said to the girl. "C'mon, honey. Say something. Tell me you'll hang in there while I come get you."

"Really? 'Hang in there?'"

"Not now, Doc."

"Where are you going?"

"Just promise me you won't let her die." Beluga ran outside, came around to the part of the building nearest where Jackleg hung inside, jammed a foot into a space between two pieces of wood and reached for another space above her head. She'd climb the wall, get to one of the vents in the roof, and pluck Jackleg through it. Easy as pie. Her thoughts circled, morbid. Good thing she hadn't had any breakfast. The extra weight was perhaps more than the derelict building would be willing to support.

The wood plank groaned under her weight, but held sturdy. So far, so good. She scraped her foot along the edge of the wall until she felt a space to wiggle out a new step, and reached higher for a handhold.

"How's she doing, doc?"

"The sooner we get her out of here the better," he yelled back.

A low keening sound touched her ears. She couldn't be sure if it was the girl or something else. Her foot slipped then and slammed her body into the side of the building as she fought to hold on. Splinters dug deep into her fingers, but she was relieved to note there wasn't any pain. Not now anyway.

"Hold on, honey. I'm almost there." She wished that speaking the words would make them true, but every step up made the distance between her and Jackleg seem that much further.

The keening sound grew higher, rhythmic, and more immediate. And it came from more than one source.

Beluga took a deep breath and drew on every reserve she had in her to push on. Another step. Another stretch of her arm with fingers scratching and clawing for a place to hold and pull herself up. And then she was there, where tin roof met walls, when she heard it.

At first it was slight, like a quiet sigh before one drifts off to sleep, but soon enough it became the restless sleep of an old man snoring fitfully enough that he awakened himself. Deep, resonate noises sprang randomly from the wood as if it had something to say but had not yet fully formed the words. The rest of the wood in the building joined in then, just as they had been joined together for all those many decades. But here and now and collectively, the wood made the choice to finally let go.

Joints separated. Random wood planks slipped easily away from one another to fall to the ground. Walls swayed ever so slightly, sagged, then slowly, so very slowly, leaned inward and invited the roof with them.

There was no chance to send a warning to those inside even though time had stopped as she knew it. The wood under her fingertips fell inward, and she followed, distanced and dispassionately as if watching someone else who looked like her, had her history, but remained a stranger even in the last moments of her life.

It was quiet.

So quiet that everything in her mind stilled and she found herself in a final moment of peace.

Chapter 14

The peace was fleeting.

The quiet that stilled Beluga's mind and distanced her from her body suddenly called to her with a riot of noise and chaos and confusion. And a rather disagreeable smell.

"Where am I?" she asked. "What happened?"

A young male face loomed into view and offered a kind smile. "You're going to be fine, ma'am."

He was gorgeous. A positively, radiantly, angelic gorgeous. And that could only mean one thing under the circumstances.

"I'm dead. I've passed to the other side."

"No, ma'am. Not this time. But I think it's safe to say that if you were a cat you would have used up one of your lives."

Cat.

"Planchette!" She tried to get up, but realized she couldn't move for some reason. "Planchette. Doc. Jackleg."

Alarm flickered across the man's face. "We have a situation here," he yelled.

Another man from the seeming army of people that busied themselves at the site squatted down by her side. "What have you got, D.B.?"

"Level of consciousness seems altered, Chief. She called out for a doctor, I'm almost sure of that, but the other things she said don't make sense."

"Planchette is my cat, you cretin."

"See what I mean?"

Someone pried open her eye and shone a bright light, then repeated the act on the other eye.

"Stop it," she said, but they ignored her.

Gorgeous or not, the kid was going down.

"Pupils equal and reactive to light. Squeeze my hand, ma'am. Squeeze it as hard as you can. There you go. Okay. You can let go now. Really. You can let go. No, I mean it. I think she's having a seizure, Chief. She won't let go."

The chief patted the young man on the shoulder. "No, son. It's not a seizure, but it is a fit—a fit of pique." He winked at Beluga.

She released the grip on the young man's hand.

He cradled his hand and eyed her with suspicion. "I don't follow you, sir. And I think my hand is broken."

"Ms. Stein, is it?" the chief asked.

"The one and only."

"I'm sure the EMT student will be glad to hear that. I'm Chief Daily."

"The smell…what's that smell? And I can't move."

"Your cat is enjoying D.B.'s tuna sandwich—"

D. B. gasped and started hyperventilating. "What? My wife made that for me."

Chief Daily smiled tightly. "Let's just say that what she lacks in lunch preparation skills, she more than makes up for in looks, and leave it at that."

Beluga twisted in place. "You gave my cat bad seafood?"

"On the contrary, Ms. Stein. Fresh sardines are Mrs. D.B.'s secret ingredient and your cat couldn't be happier."

"No. There's another smell. More pungent than Dromedary Spits."

"I think we're losing her again, Chief."

"Steady, boy."

"What about Doc? Is he okay?"

"Your friend is wandering the herb garden. Is that his car parked out front?"

"That's a yes if you're referring to the red speed machine?"

The chief nodded appreciatively. "Fine piece of machinery."

"Really fine," D.B. added. "Finest fine."

"None of us have seen anything like that in these parts before. The boys have been ogling it between their assigned duties. I have to practically push their eyes back in their heads every time they pass it."

"Testosterone poisoning will do that," she said, squirming in place. "I seem to be stuck."

"The reason you can't move is that you're on a backboard and are wearing a neck collar."

"Well, get me off and out of all this."

"It's a precaution until we can be sure there are no injuries."

"Want to shake on it, Chief?"

D.B. grimaced at the threat and backed away.

Chief Daily laughed. "I'll pass. But we strongly encourage you to stay where you are until we can get you to the hospital to be checked out. You took quite a tumble in there."

"And if I refuse statue status?"

"You'll have to sign a release."

"Bring it on."

"D.B.," the chief said, nodding to the young man who snapped open a metal encased clipboard to find the required paperwork. Velcro straps screeched open and the chief assisted Beluga to a sitting position. "How do you feel? Okay?"

She looked around at the assortment of cars, emergency vehicles, and the hordes of people combing the place. "I've been better, although I haven't seen this much drama in a long time."

"We aim to please." He pulled off the neck collar and watched her carefully.

The thought hit her then. "Where's Jackleg?" She tried to stand up but was taken by a wave of dizziness.

The chief eased her back down. "Take a few minutes to get everything stabilized. No one's in a hurry here."

"Jackleg. What happened to her?"

"I'm not sure I know who you mean."

"Jeannette Mason. The girl."

"Another team is working on her right now."

"Is she okay?"

"I suspect she's been better, too, and probably hasn't seen this kind of drama either. Certainly we've never been called to this house before or we'd have questioned the ramshackle smoke house long ago."

Beluga rubbed stiffness from her neck. "John Doe lived here."

The chief adopted a professional tone. "Yes, I understand he was a chef at the cooking school."

"Jackleg, I mean Jeannette Mason, knew him. She's probably been here before today."

"One presumes, since Miss Mason is the chef's sister."

"*Sister*?" Without blinking an eye Beluga scrutinized the chief's face. "Jackleg and Chef Doe are brother and sister?"

"Yeah. It's a small town. Everyone knew that. Well, except for the 'Jackleg' part. Hadn't heard that one before, but then I don't think she's been in town long."

"Well, that explains the photographs. Funny, I thought Jackleg and the chef were an item. You know, like lovers maybe."

"This is a small town, Ms. Stein, not a James Dickey novel."

"I see your point." The brief clarity she had when her mind stepped to attention at the brother-sister connection was now easing into partly cloudy again.

"Glad to make it."

"But that doesn't explain how Jackleg, er, Miss Mason, got hoisted up on a meat hook in an abandoned smokehouse. Or why."

"No, it doesn't. So there's plenty of work to do. Still, I don't mind saying what you did was nothing short of spectacular."

"Spectacular? Me? Maybe you should take a turn on the backboard, Chief."

"No. I mean it," he said. "We got there just in time to see it. The boys will talk about it for months. Well, when they're not talking about the car."

Beluga shook her head to clear the fog that lingered there. "I don't seem to have a whole lot of memory on the subject."

D.B. nodded. "You were something else, that's all I can say."

"Indeed," said the chief. "Like an angel coming to

Earth—"

"Or a major league player catching a tie-breaking fly ball—"

"As descriptive as that is, my dear menfolk, I could do with a few details."

The chief obliged. "You flew through the roof, snagged Miss Mason just as the hook gave out, and spun in the air so that when you hit the ground, she landed on you."

"And where, pray tell, did I land?"

The two men fell silent suddenly.

She rubbed a place in the small of her back and felt something disturbing. "I mean, aside from the hard ground."

D.B. looked away and muttered something.

"What's that, young man?"

"I said, a pile of bat guano. You might want to burn your clothes. What's left of them anyway."

"Well, that certainly clarifies the cruel smell coming from my direction and the fact I feel a distinct breeze in places that perhaps I shouldn't." She grazed her hand across what was left of her muumuu while resisting the urge to smell her fingers for an all-clear that most certainly would never come. Another thought hit her then. "How did you know we were here? That we needed help?"

"911."

"A phone call?"

"Yeah. And redirected from Atlanta of all places."

"Atlanta?"

"Yeah. Something else, huh?"

Atlanta…huh.

Darwin!

The phone was still connected from her call to Darwin to see what late-breaking news he might have uncovered on John Doe. She must have forgotten the phone was on when she plunged it into her pocket during one of Doc's Sebring moves on the road and while they explored the house, or ran through the woods to make the discovery in the smokehouse.

Digging deep among the folds of material, she circumnavigated the bulge in her pocket and was cheered the phone, at least, had survived the fall. A frantic *waah, waah, waah* ringing reached her ears long before her fingers fished the phone out. "Who's calling, please?"

This time the *waah, waah, waah* was entirely different.

"Just kidding, Darwin. Honestly, you really need to lighten up a notch lest you find yourself following in your father's footsteps. Has he been in today yet? Did he ask about me?"

The voice at the other end escalated to a screech. Beluga yanked the phone away from her ear, shot an embarrassed smile at the chief and D.B., then shooed them away while she spoke into the phone from a safe distance.

"Darwin. Darwin? Darwin, sweetheart, stop." Silence met her then and she carefully eased the phone to her ear. "You are a wonderful, kind, caring man who managed to selflessly, through long-distance, pull my bacon out of the fire—"

Another screech sounded then. She shot the phone out at arm's length and spoke to the rescue workers who had paused around her in case their skills might be needed at any moment. "High-strung, that's all. He'll be okay in a minute."

A minute passed. Two. Then another.

"Darwin, dear," she said, when it seemed hearing loss was at a minimal threat. "It was a figure of speech. No fire. And not the first sign of bacon. I took a spill, that's all. They bound me up like a mummy as a precaution, then set me free at my insistence, although I don't mind telling you that being smeared with bat guano was an unexpected asset to soliciting freedom. What? Never mind, long story. Everybody is okay, thanks to you. Well, except for Jackleg—no, you don't know her—but suffice it to say she's added a new wrinkle to the case.

"And speaking of cases, any pathology word I should know about? Yes, I know it's still early. Yes, I know you've gone out on a limb that will barely support the sling you're in. Yes, I know you have classes to attend. What? Really? So it looks compatible with toxicology. Good to know. Thanks, Darwin. You're a dream. Now I don't know what this funny sound in the phone means, but..."

She tapped the phone against her palm and raised it to her ear. "That's better. The battery? Really? These things have batteries? Go figure. What's that? No, Darwin. Please tell me you didn't. Well, undo it. Darwin? Darwin? Damn."

Doc loomed over her suddenly. "I hope you know you're going to pay for that call."

Beluga tossed the phone to him. "Why should I? The phone doesn't work."

"You escaped imprisonment at a cooking school, saved a life, and clearly have some news that may help this case. Why the sudden foul mood after all that?"

"Darwin called more than the police when all this was happening."

"So he called Tanya. So what? She could use a little fear in her life. Certainly she knows how to dole it out."

"Worse than that."

"Worse?"

"Far worse."

"How so?"

Beluga deeply massaged her temples, and would have her fingers meet in the middle of her brain if she could. "He called Olivia."

"Your daughter?"

"She's on her way."

Chapter 15

Beluga slumped further into the low-slung passenger seat of the sports car and stroked Planchette's sleek body with more than a little distraction. The light wind barely ruffled his fur, thus affording him the time to take a much needed nap while curled in her lap, for he had to know that all hell was about to break loose.

"Can't you go any slower, Doc? I mean, what's the rush?"

"Rush? You call this rushing?"

He waved a circle in the air at the sheriff's car in front of him. The officer replied with a single finger lifted from his hold on the steering wheel in acknowledgement.

"Ah. The North Georgia wave. How did we ever live before this communication?"

"Saints among us." Doc tapped the speedometer. "We can't be going more than twenty miles an hour." He glanced in the rearview mirror for the bookended part of their escort. "The state trooper behind us is yawning for God's sake. This is torture."

"Tell it."

Torture it was. Not just for the murder of a chef, the attempt on the life of the chef's sister who was now on her way to the hospital, or the director of the cooking school who kept a cluricaun around as a mischievous colleague, but also for the fact that Olivia was on her way this very minute. Or maybe she was already there. At the cooking school. Waiting. Planning.

Olivia. Did it have to be Olivia right here, right now?

Beluga loved her daughter more than anything in the world. If it hadn't been for Olivia's level head, open-mindedness, and contact in the newsprint world through a crime writer disturbingly named Squint, the ugly matter of murder on the set of a low budget horror film might never have been solved. But as mothers and daughters are wont to do—at least this mother and daughter—there remained an undercurrent of personal wounds. The wounds completely healed and yet were too willingly reopened again during frequent circular arguments.

Olivia knew all too well her mother's idiosyncrasies and tolerated most of them. Maturity and distance went a long way toward that compromise. She was thinking, of course, of Olivia. Beluga herself still waited patiently for some degree of maturity and didn't mind a bit that it only occasionally showed itself when the situation demanded. That, unfortunately, was part of the problem. For while the two of them enjoyed each other's company, and Beluga still kept a room just for her daughter, the fact of the matter was the two of them could only be together for short bursts of time in the same house.

Or the same town. Sometimes even the same country.

Doc pounded the steering wheel. "This is ridiculous. We're almost standing still."

And they were. She and Olivia, that was. Two

167

intelligent, well-educated, personable women: one a biology professor when she wasn't tapping into the metaphysical world, the other a...a...well, a journalist for now until she figured out what else she might want to try, and they couldn't have a meaningful conversation about meaningful topics if their lives depended on it. By meaningful Beluga meant getting to know each other rather than, say, hiding behind the topics of politics and global warning. Or if the cheese served on fast food burgers was real or some imitation-processed-artificial orange-colored foodstuff. Beluga held hope for the former since a good cheeseburger was one on her list of basic food group necessities along with caffeine, nicotine, and a hot toddy or two.

She and Olivia loved each other, no doubt about it. But frankly, sometimes they didn't like each other very much. Especially when Olivia dug in her heels and exhibited a deep stubborn streak. For the life of her, Beluga had no idea where that unfortunate trait came from. She smiled then. Well, she could guess. Some people would say the apple didn't fall far from the tree.

So the two had reached a truce of sorts. Olivia would be her own woman—against everything Beluga's maternal instincts told her was right, fair, natural, and legal—and Beluga would live her life as she saw fit. Too bad they couldn't agree on a similar lifestyle, lock-stepping together with common interests through the years as partners in crime. No, not in crime. There was far too much of that going around as it was. But maybe that was the key. Olivia had helped once, now maybe she could help again. That would be the common ground connecting them.

It was worth a shot.

"Damn it," Doc said, causing Planchette to open one eye and stare. "We could walk faster than this."

"You can walk twenty miles an hour? Perhaps the Olympic Committee should pay a visit. I can make a call."

"They wouldn't answer your call. Mine, maybe. It's not right, going so slow in a car like this. I should be gathering bugs in my teeth and loving every minute."

"Trust me when I say I hope to never have that experience."

"Certainly you won't this afternoon."

"Oh, but I came close this morning."

He glanced in the rear view mirror, muttered under his breath, and nodded at her. "Out of your funk now?"

"Was it that obvious?"

"You are many things, Beluga Stein, but subtle is not one of them."

"I beg to differ."

"Beg away. It won't do one whit of good. Settled things in your mind about Olivia?"

She shrugged. "As best as possible when one person makes a decision for two. The rubber will hit the road when I see her."

"Well, there's damn little rubber burning up the highways now. Just a slow burn I have working in the pit of my stomach."

"Cars capable of movement at the speed of light can't be everything, Doc."

"Maybe not, but it sure makes things infinitely more fun. No, the slow burn in my belly is about something else entirely."

Beluga swiveled in the tight seat and brought

Planchette instantly out of his reverie. "You found something."

"Maybe."

"Spill it."

"What's it worth to you?"

"Look, Doc, I'm tired, vulnerable, preparing for an inquisition from my daughter, and I'm betting Petula Brock would love to have more muffin target practice."

"You are a wicked woman."

"And proud of it. So let loose and be quick about it."

"First, I found this." He reached into a pocket and produced foliage wrapped in a handkerchief.

"Is it…?"

"Lily of the Valley. I found it in the herb garden."

"But it's poisonous. Why would a chef, an expert on this kind of thing, have that growing next to edible herbs?"

"It was a new addition. Recent. Very recent. And undetectable except to a trained eye."

Beluga stared at him. "The plant was a plant?"

"To paraphrase a friend of mine, 'I'm not saying, I'm just saying.'"

"Could it have been put there after his death?"

"It's possible. Even likely, by the look of the disturbed soil."

"With the idea that eventually a trained eye would find it?"

"Yep." Doc stole a look in the rearview mirror, a side mirror, and the other side mirror, as if he were hoping that a reason to speed would materialize.

"We're going fast enough, Doc. Let it go."

"Right. Zero to sixty in twenty minutes. Who

doesn't like that kind of g-force?"

"Any chance those with little training in such matters of flora might see the chef's death as, say, a suicide rather than murder."

"Possible."

"But unlikely, don't you think? Even though the report isn't in, Darwin says the chef's death is compatible with the toxicology of such a plant. Still, why suffer through that kind of death when he had to know there were other things less painful? Besides, nothing else in his background points to him as the sort to take his own life. He was renovating his house, he loved what he did, the students adored him, and we know someone else had been in the house recently. You saw the food in the refrigerator."

"I did. So did you. On to point two."

"Okay."

"Jackleg."

"Yes?"

"Think about it, Beluga."

"I can do little else."

"She was drunk when you saw her before?"

"As a skunk."

"On alcohol?"

"We had a party. She had a drink in her hand."

"Are you sure?"

"I think I am." Beluga racked her mind to remember the details, but they were murky at best. "I was on the phone with Darwin. Someone handed me a Dromedary Spit, I gave it back. Jackleg drank it. That was the drink I saw in her hand."

"Dromedary Spit?"

"Long story, worse drink. She sat next to me, well,

more like she leaned into me, and started talking. Tanya made us more Dromedary Spits, but if I remember it right, we never got around to drinking them."

"So you only saw Jackleg have one drink?"

"She had to have had more I didn't see. She was already drunk. Unless…"

"Yes?"

"Maybe she didn't have a lot to drink. Maybe she only had a little, and there was something else put in the drinks she did have. Something that didn't belong there."

"That's what I'm wondering. Because, quite frankly—"

"Drunk is one thing," Beluga said, "but being pliable enough to be dragged through a dorm room to a car, driven to a remote location, then suspended on a hook in a smokehouse might take more than a few drinks. Even if they were Dromedary Spits."

"Which brings me to my next thought—"

"What kind of strength does it take to do all those things, and who commands that kind of strength?"

"Beluga, can you not finish my thought before I get it out?"

"It's a gift."

"It's a pain."

"You say potato…"

"Not if I can help it."

The car, if it was possible, slowed down even further as they approached the entrance to the cooking school complex. The sheriff's car in front turned at an angle and stopped. This was an indication to Doc and his passengers they should turn into the school driveway, which they did with great reluctance.

"Here we go," Beluga said with a low moan.

Doc looked into the rear view window. "The state trooper has taken off. At a respectable speed I might add."

"Why shouldn't he? We're back within the prison gates and there appear to be plenty of people waiting for us."

"Yup. There goes the sheriff, too. I believe he'll overtake the trooper in mere seconds."

"Oh no."

"What?"

"Look. Everyone's there. Tanya, Olivia, Petula Brock readying a muffin, Ned Niblett, the cooking students, and even the officer who took the note I found in the dorm room."

The note supposedly written by Jackleg.

Now there was another note, Beluga knew suddenly. It was in the same handwriting, in the same style, and close enough she could almost feel it within her grasp. All she had to do was find it, and more importantly, she had to find a way to make sense out of it.

Doc pulled a piece of paper out of his breast pocket. "Was it a note like this?"

Beluga snatched it from his hand. "Well, yes. Very much like this. And I can only venture a guess where you got it."

"I daresay you'd be right, too."

She read the note again, then spoke to him out of the corner of her mouth while she surveyed the crowd lest they suspect something. "Which brings me decisively to point three…"

Planchette stood up on Beluga's lap, eyes wide, tail

twitching, and considered the note in Beluga's hand and the gathering that awaited their arrival. A low rumble formed deep in his chest.

She stroked the cat from head to tail and leaned in close. "Are you thinking what I'm thinking, boy?"

He winked. Once. Then dove into the foot well of the car.

From the corner of her mouth again: "We have to go back, Doc."

"Don't toy with me."

"I would never do anything like that. I may regret what I'm about to say, but I have no choice but to say it anyway." She turned to him and let loose like she was at a game during the last seconds of a tied game. "Let's see what this baby can do."

Chapter 16

Doc pushed through the undergrowth to where the smokehouse now sat in tumbled ruins.

Beluga followed at a significantly slower pace. Similar to stepping on solid ground after spending a week on a ship plowing through turbulent seas, she found her footing to be shaky and indecisive. Maybe it was because the drive here in the car launched her inner ear out somewhere along Booger Way. Her stomach undoubtedly left her body through violent osmosis on Holler Road, and she could only hope that whatever body part was shaken out on All The Trout You Can Eat Boulevard was one she wouldn't miss or that was on an eligible transplant list.

Her hair had become stiff as straw after a summer of broiling heat, and now stuck straight out from the back of her head as the result of a g-force that would remain forever unrecorded. The look, she feared, might be permanent.

Planchette had fared little better, having dug his claws into something static and deep within the foot well. He had spat to make it clear his situation was completely unacceptable and she had better do something. Quick. After a great deal of thought over eight seconds, give or take, Beluga's only rescue plan was to crawl as far as possible toward his confinement to perform the Planchette extrication; but the tiny space in the tiny sports car was painfully designed to counter any such rescue.

The seats in the sports car were small to begin with, and due to the challenge of the tight leg room Beluga figured few in the *Mammalia* class would fit. Particularly a middle-aged mammal who never turned down junk food, or what she called it, "yet another important food group." Explanation or excuses aside, she wriggled, squirmed, cursed until she ran out of words, and hoped no one noticed her feet and rump in the air, and the upper part of her body wedged under the dash. She would never hear the end of it—so to speak—if her biology students saw her in such a compromising position.

She pushed the air out of her lungs as best she could, moved another inch, and came face-to-face with Planchette. With little breath left she squeaked out what she hoped were words of comfort. "It's okay, my handsome boy."

Perhaps it was because her voice sounded like exhaled helium, or maybe it was the consoling words themselves. One thing was sure, he would never act like an overindulged, self-absorbed, attention-seeking, schemer, beast-cat from the underworld. It simply wasn't in his nature.

Without so much as a blink of his eye, Planchette gracefully withdrew his claws from what was a trap mere seconds ago. He touched her nose with his, then squeezed his way to freedom under her armpit with a final caress to her face by the tip of his tail.

"Planchette! Don't you walk away from me, young man. You come back here." She twisted ever so slightly in one direction while her legs circled and kicked as if an unhinged dancer occupied the passenger seat, rather than the top of her body like normal people. "Come back here right *now*."

Doc snickered. "Are we having some agility issues?"

The frantic kicking stopped. A second passed, two. She leisurely crossed her ankles.

"All is fine here. You?"

"Not bad. Not bad at all."

She heard a series of clicks, followed by another lengthy snicker. "I know you're not taking pictures."

"I'm shocked. And hurt at the accusation."

"Then get me out of here."

He pushed, pulled, shoved, yanked, and insisted she follow his lead to add to the effort.

"I'm trying, damn it."

"Try harder."

They heaved and ho'd until suddenly she was free, with a sound like a cork popping out of a champagne bottle.

Beluga fell out of the car's open door, and took the opportunity to stay down for a breather. "Well, that happened."

Doc wrenched his shirt free from his trousers to wipe his forehead and neck from an inundation of sweat.

"We shall never speak of this again. Right, Doc?"

"Get up. We've got things to do."

"Give me a hand, would you?"

Doc pulled her to her feet.

"How about you, Planchette? Are you coming?"

Green eyes watched her intently. One pyramidal ear swiveled like an array radio telescope.

"All right. Suit yourself."

She couldn't blame Planchette for passing on the revisit to the smokehouse. Instead, he was taking time to groom himself into some semblance of his former self. Perhaps he would take a second look around the ruined smokehouse once he had sufficiently stretched his legs after the sports car confinement. After all, he had four legs to her two, so the stakes were a little higher. Unfortunately—her jaw tightened at the realization—it appeared some characteristics of an overindulged, self-absorbed, attention-seeking, schemer, beast-cat from the underworld *was* in his nature. Thank the heavens Planchette was on her side.

Beluga followed Doc as he made his final push through the undergrowth to where the smokehouse now sat in tumbled ruins.

"What a mess," Doc said, looking at the wrecked building.

Calling it "a mess" was an understatement at best. She reached his side and stared.

"It has a long way to go before being a mess. So where did you find the note?"

"It floated out of her clothing just before you came through the roof. I barely made it out of there."

The note. Same as before with the misspelled name and the handwriting that was anyone's but Jackleg's. But the message was similar; a confession to the murder of a chef. This time, though, the note spoke with a hint of remorse and an action plan that explained why she had no choice but to kill herself by dragging her drugged body to a smokehouse and hoisting herself high into the air without benefit of animal, mineral, or vegetable assistance.

Yeah, right.

"There's more here than meets my eye." Beluga spied a circuitous route of sorts the rescue workers took to free Jackleg and her from the fallen wreckage, and followed the path.

"Watch your step. You could get hurt."

Watch her step? She could barely feel her legs, but right now that might be for the better. "I still can't figure out how Jackleg got up there in the first place. Help me look."

"Does it really matter? I mean, the authorities will only be minutes behind us, and there's got to be more important things to spend our time on. Besides, this place has got tetanus written all over it. Or worse." He backed up a step. "Mission over."

"Help me look, Doc, or I'll wait, wait however long it takes, because I know where you live and you have to sleep eventually."

"*I* have a few photos your university's yearbook staff might be interested in."

Beluga chose her final threat carefully. "One day, when you least expect it, your precious death-defying, road hazard, red speed machine will be gone and you'll never see it again. Ever."

Doc gasped. "You wouldn't."

"I would."

"You couldn't."

"I have a few friends in, you know, some places. So, I could, I would, and I will with utmost pleasure."

"I think you may be despicable, Beluga Stein."

"When you make up your mind, let me know. In the meantime, pick up that end of the tin roof piece and be quick about it."

He did. One after another was lifted and tossed, and those were followed by splintered wood and ultimately to a still and rather solid beam that held a metal device.

"Finally," Doc said, straightening up and rubbing the small of his back. "The mystery has been solved."

Beluga looked at the pulley. "Were that true I could go home to Emerson, and a buffet of fast food set out on top of their grease-stained take-out bags. You know, I really need to rethink this entire psychic investigator thing. The price may be too high. But until I get a solid series of mental impressions that make sense, I'll settle for irrefutable facts, as scarce as they are."

"She was hoisted up using the pulley. You'd think we'd have noticed that old thing before."

"We were a tad distracted."

"Had to be the pulley."

"Wouldn't that take rope? And a good bit of it?"

"Sure it would. But rope is transportable. Evidence gone as quick as it arrived. On the other hand, a fixed pulley on a beam high in the air doesn't lend itself to portability."

"But it does swivel." She kicked it with her foot to prove her point. "It appears to have been close enough that transferring Jackleg to the hooks wouldn't be too difficult. Still, wouldn't that command some strength by a perp?"

"You've forgotten your science background, dear."

"I've forgotten many things, Doc. How to stand still without swaying being the newest among them."

"With enough rope, and the use of the pulley, someone even much smaller than your victim would be perfectly capable of getting her up there. It would take some time, but it's definitely doable."

"Great. So now we know how it was done, but it could have been anyone of just about any size. Unless…"

"You know what? I almost saw the wheels turning in your head."

"That's because my inner ear is gone, and it's a straight shot."

"You were saying?"

"How did the perp get Jackleg to the smokehouse in the first place? The pulley couldn't help with that, and it's a bit of walk from the house. And she was impaired, at least to some degree." Beluga climbed out of the debris and scouted the periphery. "No drag marks. The underbrush is clean except where we and the rescue workers came in."

"Unless…"

Beluga looked at him. "Now who's got a few wheels turning?"

"Unless she was dropped in from above."

"What?"

"You know, like from a helicopter or something."

"Yeah." Beluga snorted. "You can throw a stick and hit a helicopter owner in these parts. Since air transportation really comes in handy during those pesky traffic jams after a high school football game, everyone around here owns one."

"I do."

She stared at him and cocked an eyebrow. "Of course you do."

"No. Really. I do."

"Okay," she said, clearly doubting him.

"I do."

"Then you've left me no choice. I'm arresting you for the attempted murder of Jackleg. Get in the car. I'm driving this time."

"You can't arrest me. Besides, I didn't try to kill that girl, and you know it."

"I also know you're insane."

"That may be, but I do own a helicopter—it was an impulse buy—and the possibility she was dropped in from above shouldn't be ruled out. Besides, you're the one who's insane if you think for a skinny minute you're driving my car."

"Think, Doc. There's no indication of the underbrush disrupted by propellers, and no one's reported any low flying aircraft or crop circles. Not that I'd mind a bit seeing one. A crop circle, that is. Trust me when I say that in these small towns, where gossip is considered a profession, someone would notice a helicopter. Hell, my neighbors alert the media when I don't bathe for a couple of days."

"You don't bathe every day?"

She was on a roll and chose to ignore him. "And there's no way she could have been lowered through the vents in the smokehouse. They're too small. You'd have a better chance of convincing me of the absurd if you told me she simply materialized here via some sort of hoo-doo, or that she'd been brought up through a secret passageway in the floor." She stopped with the thought.

As if rehearsed to perfect their timing, the two locked gazes, then as one turned their attention to the pile of debris.

"No way," Beluga said.

"It can't be," Doc added.

"Are we standing on hollow ground?"

"Hard to say, as it were."

"Get moving, Doc. We have a lot of smokehouse to clear before we find what we're looking for."

"Again? What are we looking for?"

"We'll know it when we see it. At least I hope so."

It was work, hard work. One piece after another of tin roof after splintered wood was heaved to one side as they searched the ground for any sign of a door to a hidden passageway. Nothing. The ground was hard packed soil and clay and—.

Beluga cocked her head at the muddled sound, but a couple of bars in a tinny rendition of a Bach concerto was unmistakable. "What is that?"

Doc patted his pockets and pulled out another phone with a shrug. "Backup, just in case."

"You're taking a call now? This minute? And Bach alerted you?" Beluga was incredulous at this turn of events. "Have you no shame?"

"None to speak of. Besides, this is my emergency line. Old patients in need of a sane opinion, delivery time of an antiquity. You know, that kind of thing." He flipped open the phone and answered. "Doc here."

Beluga checked her annoyance and went on with the mission as planned. No visual signs of access to a secret passageway was evident, but then the site was pretty well disturbed. She proceeded with a backup plan for a discovery by starting with a stomp, then a series of stomps, then a little dance of stomping. A creak sounded under her foot. She paused momentarily, rocked a little on the place in question, nodded to herself, then stomped up a storm to clear away the dirt, debris, and guano quicker, and more acceptably aesthetic than she could on hands and knees. It worked, but not quite in the way she had in mind.

A loud crack split the air.

Surprise flickered across her face for a second, and then she dropped. The floor of the smokehouse disappeared in the blink of an eye as she fell, yet everything slowed as if she was running in knee-high ocean waves. Doc's single syllable words stretched out unbroken and relentless, then came to a protracted stop.

A beat passed. Two. She caught her breath and spoke from deep in the earth. Or at least from just below the surface of the smokehouse. "I'm okay."

Doc leaned over the rim of the hole. "I'll try," he said into the phone, "but she seems to be under the weather at the moment."

Beluga squirmed her way back up so that her head and shoulders rose above ground.

He handed over the phone. "It's for you."

Streaks of mud ran along one side of her face and plastered her hair to her head. "I think I found a passageway."

"I can see that."

"Don't know where it goes yet."

"In good time."

"But it's safe to say there are no bottles of wine anywhere to be seen. Not that there's room where I am, even for a split."

"Be still my heart. Know, however, that I should be alerted immediately should any vintage Chateau Margaux, St-Emilion or Petrus Pomerol surfaces."

"Who are they?"

"Obviously no one with whom you'd be familiar."

He wagged the phone at her. "Will you take the call or shall I say you're in a meeting with the mole people?"

"Who is it?"

"Olivia."

Oh boy.

Working one arm free in this tight place to get the phone was hard enough, but she knew somehow that talking to her daughter right now would be even more of a challenge. "Hello?"

While the *waah, waah, waah* this time was definitely feminine, it was similar to the call with Darwin in that there was plenty of concern hidden behind anger.

"Who is this?" Beluga joked, then winced at the hair-curling pitch of Olivia's response.

Damn. Would she ever learn that most people didn't find that joke funny when they were worried?

"I'm sorry, baby. It's just that—" Beluga rolled her eyes at Doc. "Yes, I'm aware of the trouble I've caused. Yes, I know it doesn't look good with the authorities. Speaking of which, where are they? I thought a SWAT team would be here about now. Really? That's not good. You're right, dear, I think even less of that. I've got to say that's not a stellar motivation for me to come back."

Planchette appeared then. Eyes wide, ears folded back, the tip of his tail twitching ever so slightly, he took in the scene, then looked deep into her eyes.

"Gotta go, hon. Look's like something may be up. Yes, I'll come back. Sooner or later. See you, sweetie. Love and kisses." She tossed the phone to Doc. "What's on your mind, Planchette?"

The cat sniffed around the edge of the hole, then

scratched in the dirt.

"Everything all right?" Doc asked.

"Sure. If you call the police putting me on their most wanted for-now list, a cluricaun running amok at the cooking school, and my daughter threatening to put me in a home, all right."

"There's a cluricaun at the cooking school?" Doc cocked his head to one side and barely nodded. "Does it have a solid background in French cuisine? Because, you know, we could use someone who understands the nuances of a fine consommé." He raised one eyebrow. "What's a cluricaun anyway?"

"Olivia wants to put me in a home and all you can do is ask about the black sheep of the leprechaun family?"

"So that's a no to consommé?" He leaned close to her face. "Relax, Beluga. No self respecting home would consider you, so put that out of your mind."

She took a deep breath then, and a little tension eased from her body. "Thanks, Doc. I can almost always count on you to say the right thing."

Planchette sped up his scratching of dirt around the hole.

"Now if Olivia had said 'institution' I'd be a little worried."

"There's where you made your mistake, Doc. You couldn't stop with at least a half kindness in my time of need?"

"It's in my nature to weigh the odds. To prepare for the worse, if necessary."

"Then prepare for this. If I'm put away, you'll be in the next room."

"Spite is most unbecoming."

"And Tanya will be your roommate."

"Now you're just being cruel."

Planchette stopped suddenly, looked wildly around as if an idea had suddenly struck, then plunged his body deftly along Beluga's and disappeared into the hole like Alice's white rabbit.

"Really? We're repeating your car escape! Come back, boy. Planchette, where are you?" She dropped back into the hole, but couldn't see a thing. "He's gone. I don't know where he's going." She twisted and popped back up from the tight space with a creak from the wood frame around her.

That creak jogged her memory of another creak from wood. One she had heard that very day, but from where?

"Or maybe I do know where he's going. Get me out of here."

"We may need Houdini for this extrication, Beluga. Or some lubricant."

"Very funny." She planted her hands on the ground and pushed up. "Hurry with the help. I don't want to keep Planchette waiting."

"Honestly, Beluga, I'm not a miracle worker."

By rocking back and forth, and a repeat push-me pull-you encounter like with Doc's car, she finally emerged from the hole in a kneeling position.

"You look like a semi-finalist in a mud wrestling competition."

"I'd squint at you in a menacing manner if my eyes didn't feel like they were glued open." She cupped her hands around her mouth and yelled. "Last chance, Planchette. Are you coming or not?" Her center of gravity suddenly shifted and threatened to drop her back into the hole when she was yanked to her feet.

"The next time you fall in you're on your own."

A small smile turned up the corners of her mouth. "Why, Doc, I didn't know you had that kind of strength."

"We can talk about my body building at a later date. Right now that wood under your feet sounds like it could go anytime."

"Beg your pardon?" She listened as the floor of the smokehouse, or perhaps it was indeed one end of a passageway, screeched, groaned and— "Oh. *Oh.*" Creaked! Of course. "What are you waiting for, Doc? I know where we can find Planchette."

"Hold on there, old girl. I used up all my adrenaline trying to save you…"

But she was moving too fast to hear anything else he said. It was as if the mud covering her body was a super power that parted dense foliage, thwarted the sting of thorny things, and pushed revenge to the back of her mind when Doc called her "old girl." She brushed against the dense foliage of the herb garden and carried with her the scents of sweet pineapple sage, warming chocolate mint, woodsy rosemary and gentle lavender. Breathless enough that she thought she'd never feel air in her lungs again, she pushed open the door to Chef Doe's cabin, trotted into the kitchen area, and leaned heavily against the refrigerator while waiting for Doc to arrive.

Doc strode in after what seemed a couple of hours. "That is the most extraordinary garden I've ever been witness to. What a wonderful collection, and so carefully cared for. I wish I had known this unique chef."

Beluga rose up on tiptoe, then came down as flatfooted and heavy as possible. "You've forgotten why we're here, *old boy*." Up, down. Up again, then down. "Hear that?"

"Hear what?"

"Right here, by the refrigerator." Up on her toes, down full-footed.

"You mean my patience starting to crack?"

"No, Doc. The floor starting to crack. There's something under here, or rather, there might not be too much directly under here at all."

A piercing feline yowl split the air. Beluga sprung to her toes, then settled down with a deep sigh of relief.

"Now *that* I heard." Doc leaned close to the floor. "Not to worry Master Planchette. We're here. Help me move the refrigerator, Beluga."

"Help you? Planchette is my cat. You can help me." A high-pitched, elongated sound came from below her feet and could have shattered crystal had there been any around. Beluga gestured at the floor. "Okay, okay. I'm sorry. You don't belong to me, I belong to you."

"If she's a bother, you can always move in with me," Doc announced to the floor. A beat passed. Then another. "I believe he's purring."

"Spare me your wishful thinking, Doc. Can we move this appliance, please?"

With what seemed to be the new routine in her life, they pushed, pulled, heaved, ho'd, and even twisted the refrigerator now and then just for a little something different.

"Well, I'll be," Doc said, stroking his chin.

"Don't just stand there. Let's do what any warm-blooded, snoopy-types would do—with or without prompting from a testy cat—we open the trap door."

Rusted hinges screamed and dropped a sprinkling of rust. The two of them looked in. Jutting out from inside the tunnel wall was a particularly nasty splinter holding a torn piece of chef jacket material, and two steps down sat a cranky cat with wide green eyes that swiftly narrowed into ticked off slits.

"Planchette! Come here, you handsome man." Beluga never tired of seeing his face, especially at first sight when she had worried about him.

Planchette emerged from the tunnel with his ears half-flattened, a clear indication he was unhappy at the delay to release him from the cool dark space, and proceeded to leap out and lope about with a grayed and fluttering paper tenuously stuck to his flank.

Doc gasped with recognition and followed Planchette, while snatching at the elusive paper and speaking in forced conciliatory and soothing tones, that is, baby talk. "Who's my little man? You are, that's who. Don't you want to stop for a minute? A second? Sure you do."

Planchette looked over his shoulder and loped a little faster. Doc quickened his pace. Planchette zigged one way, but Doc countered. Planchette countered Doc's zig with a zag until the two of them appeared to run in circles. Beluga thought her eyes would simply roll around in her head like dice in a cup if she tried to watch them another second.

"Oh, for pity's sake. Stop it you two."

To her amazement they did. She picked up Planchette, held him against her chest, and scratched his ears. The piece of paper finally loosed itself from Planchette's fur and fell off, and the immediate drama was over for the two of them. Doc was a different matter altogether.

Caught on cool air currents rising from the tunnel, the paper floated toward the kitchen floor, only to be rudely snatched away from a graceful landing and brought to his face for a closer look. Doc stared at the paper and seemed to hold his breath for what seemed like a good fifteen minutes by Beluga's estimate.

"Doc?"

He mouthed the words on the paper over and over, then stumbled back a step as if suddenly weak. Doc reached blindly behind himself to grab the back of a kitchen chair to remain steady, yet never missed a word of the silent recitation. Not once did he utter even a hint of sound, or reveal a shadow of worry in lines on his face. The only thing that changed was the slowing tempo of unvoiced words as if he were in a dance of seduction.

If Beluga didn't know better, she'd say he was in an active state of... love swooning. Eww. Worse, that thought, the images that followed, was burned forever in her mind.

"Hey!" She snapped her fingers inches from his face. "Hey! Cut it out."

He shook his head as if awakening from an unexpected nap, then glared at her.

"Would that the ME looked at me the way you look at that piece of paper. Care to share?"

"I would not. This, dear lady," he said, holding up a label and pulling it back quicker than an expert-level speed reader, "is a partial label belonging to a bottle of vintage Margaux from the Haut-Médoc district of Bordeaux. Vintage. I intend to find the bottle where the rest of the label is hopefully affixed."

He bolted down the steps into the tunnel. Motion-activation lights followed him and turned the tunnel from midnight into diffused early morning.

Beluga followed him by easing onto the first step, careful not to knock herself out on the edge of the trap door or tear her clothes on the lethal-looking splinter that held a swatch of chef attire. She reached the floor of the tunnel, looked up to see Planchette's face gazing down at her, and blew him a kiss. "Thanks for connecting the dots from the smokehouse to here, sweetie. Well done."

He winked, then disappeared from view.

"You have got to see this, Beluga." Doc stage-whispered from a nearby intersection. "Remarkable." He beckoned to her, then gestured at the various passages that branched off from the main tunnel as if he were directing traffic. "Chambertin, Montrachet, St-Emilion. Absolutely remarkable" He stumbled to one side and put his hand on his forehead. "I think I blacked out for a moment." One step into a corridor and he was back to reverence. "Languedoc. So many Grand Crus. Not near enough time…"

Beluga nodded in what she hoped was appropriate appreciation, but in truth she didn't hear half of what he said, concerned as she was about more important matters. The tunnel was not quite tall enough for Doc's impressive stature, or comfortably wide enough in many places for her. So an accident in here could prove dangerous. Or, if exceedingly unlucky, just illegal.

This tunnel—or rather noteworthy wine cellar—had clearly been here for a long time. A very long time. From the remnants of rusted equipment found in a heap, it might have been used for making "shine" at one time. Moonshine production and distribution would at least account for the existence of the tunnel and for one end of it cleverly opening into a seemingly innocent smokehouse. Still, the underground labyrinth, at least this part, appeared to be in unusually good shape.

"Remarkable," said Doc.

Indeed it was.

Chapter 17

Beluga Stein's Diary

I am writing this addendum while in a sports car that, theoretically, can move fast enough to turn back time. Yet my handwriting comes out perhaps more legible than ever thanks to the speed, or rather lack of speed, that Doc has chosen for our trip back to the school.

There is no police escort to slow us down this time, much to my disappointment since I thought, or hoped anyway, that we were still interesting enough to be pursued fugitives from justice. But worse, our speed is such that a family of ducks can waddle back to the school faster than we're going, not to mention a family of ducks being whole-heartedly pursued by Planchette.

Not that Planchette would ever do such a thing. Being a feline of fine upstanding morals—and an incredibly talented sleuth in his own right—Planchette remains passive in the face of all things wild and moving in the natural world. Perhaps it's because an unfortunate encounter could disrupt his sleep or cause a retaliatory injury that could disrupt his sleep. I don't know.

But come to think of it, he doesn't much care for disturbed sleep patterns from things in the unnatural world either, like, say, paranormal events. Well, except for my psychic gifts which, frankly, he accepts quite gracefully, although not with the enthusiasm and appreciation he takes for his own gifts. Is it just me or has anyone else noticed the superior attitude cats can adopt for themselves? Hmm. Anyway, he remains comfortable with his chosen lifestyle as observer and sleeper.

Much like he's sleeping now. Curled in my lap, a handsome arm draped casually over his stunning face, he's actively banking sleep. I've seen this behavior before in the face of adversity, and I don't mind telling you it gives me pause. For I know his deep sleep right now means he's shoring up for the fury of hell that undoubtedly awaits us. And in perhaps more ways than can be counted on every one of his gorgeous toes.

That's not to say he doesn't have other assets as well. He has many, not the least of which is the ability to issue occasional ear-bleeding alerts as necessary.

Alerts much like the almost deafening yowl he let out from under the refrigerator in Chef Doe's cabin portending the existence of a tunnel. The very same tunnel, I should add, that delivered one shockingly expensive vintage bottle of wine as proof of a heretofore mostly unknown world class cellar. The proof was even now wrapped in all available spare clothing—I refused to give Doc my Egypt-themed muumuu—and now the prized wine sat in Doc's lap. At least he thought it was a prized bottle. It could have held cranberry juice for all I knew, especially since the kidnapped bottle was sans most of the label. Thus the reason for our just above idle speed back to the cooking school. But I digress.

The tunnel was creepy and fascinating at the same

time, but what drew my eye for closer inspection was that it was in the process of being shored up. Renovated.

And there was only one man who would know the ins and outs, as it were, of this project.

****

"Burton Smith."

"What's that?" Doc eased the car around a small oak branch in the road and glanced fearfully at the bottle of wine in his lap. "Did you say something?"

"I said, the clock chimes at midnight and let the dancing begin."

"Yeah. Okay." He said this clearly without benefit of listening while surveying the road for any other lethal obstacles that might threaten the wine. "Me, too."

"I want to talk to Burton Smith."

"Sure thing. Anytime now. Clocks."

Planchette opened an eye and looked at her.

"That's right, boy. Doc has gone away for awhile. Maybe he'll come back someday a better man."

"Me, too," Doc said.

She scratched Planchette behind the ears. "I don't think you met Burton Smith, but he was the one who saw Chef Doe the night before he was murdered. He's done some work out there in the cabin and I think he might be very helpful to us now. That is, if Tanya hasn't gotten to him first. Honestly, I think she may be the first ever case of female testosterone poisoning."

Planchette yawned wide enough that Beluga could almost count the number of his teeth.

"Like you he's not much of a talker, the Smith fellow. So that's going to be a problem."

"Problem?" Doc's voice reached an octave Beluga

was sure didn't occur naturally to him. He tapped the brake. "What problem? Do you see something in the road?"

"Go back to your meditative state, Doc, or whatever state you're in and let me figure this out."

He stroked the bottle and visibly calmed a notch. "Don't want anything to happen to this baby. It's been around this long...."

"How can you be sure that what you think is in the bottle is really what's in the bottle...really?"

"You want to try that one again, this time in a recognizable language?"

"You know what I mean. There's no label on it."

"Planchette's label matched perfectly the marks where it would have been on the bottle. It's the real thing. No doubt about it."

"You're sure, Doc? Really sure?"

"The markings on the top of the cork promise paradise as well.

"Well, as long as it's paradise." Beluga turned to him. "What are you going to do with it anyway?"

Doc swallowed hard. "Hadn't really thought about it."

"Liar. You've been doing nothing else since you found it in the wine cellar. You know it's evidence, don't you?"

"For what? The only crime that's been committed is that this and the others have been sitting underground for who knows how long without benefit of an appreciative audience."

"Not so."

"What do you mean?"

"The pattern in the wine racks."

"I hadn't noticed."

"You were a tad, er, overly enthusiastic, Doc."

"I was, at most, preoccupied."

"Enthusiastically preoccupied enough that I thought you'd lose control of certain body functions."

"There will be no further discussion on this point. Move on."

"Moving on. The bottles appeared to have been systematically removed from the wine racks. The one's nearest the trapdoor entrance were empty, and they were being emptied from other racks proximally to the door and in a vertical manner. Top to bottom. The racks beyond were completely filled. Not a missing bottle anywhere."

"True enough," Doc said, with an unmistakable tone of reverie.

"Besides, how do you know Chef Doe wasn't appreciative? He's the one who owned all the booze."

Doc's mouth popped open in what appeared to be a scream, yet the sound he made, if any, was one only dogs could hear. He shuddered. "You...you...you. Have. Spoken. Blasphemy. By using such a word."

"What word? Booze?"

"Quiet! Still your lips from the use of that vulgar word right now, or I will stop this car until some semblance of civility can be resumed."

"We're practically at a standstill as it is. Besides, you're missing the big picture in your addled state of mind. The crime was murder and this bottle, appreciative audience or not, might be the key to everything. In fact, I'm counting on it."

"Why, pray tell?"

"Because I'm stuck with a scarcity of suspects

otherwise, and the hair on the back of my neck is standing up."

"A good barber could take care of that."

"And get rid of my psychic antennae? I don't think so."

"What else have you got? I mean, besides tingly neck hair?"

"Now who's being crude? Let me have that bottle."

"No way."

"C'mon, Doc. I need to touch it, hold it, and see if I get anything."

"If anything happens to it…"

"I'll buy you another one."

"Best of luck in that endeavor. If you can even find one you might have to mortgage your house to get it. I know what biology professors get paid."

"Not near enough, that's for sure. But that's neither here nor there. Give up the bottle, or I'll stomp my foot on the accelerator and push this car up to a life-threatening twenty-five."

"You wouldn't! And, as you well know, you couldn't. This car's not designed for more than two feet in this space at a time and mine are already here."

Beluga softened her voice. "You know I'm going to win. I always do."

His eyebrows rose.

"Well, usually I win. Most of the time. Will you just hand it over and be done with it?"

He did. Grudgingly, by the looks of him.

She took the bundled bottle, carefully unwrapped it from all the spare clothing, and settled it deep in her hands. There was nothing at first, just the coolness of glass and the gentle settling of liquid within. And then, after a moment or two, there was…nothing.

"Damn."

"Lose your touch?"

Her hands warmed. The tingling in her neck moved down her arms and settled in her fingertips. Fire ignited there, spread to her palms, and turned her hands deep red. Then the images came. From where, she couldn't be sure, but they were there just the same. One after another in rapid succession, they flitted across her mind's eye as if she were staring into a cinemascope after a nickel had been dropped into the coin slot.

The wine funneled into a bottle. The bottle corked. Sitting. Waiting.

A voyage many miles to one destination, then to another and another.

A callused hand reaching into a box to place the bottle in a rack, within a tunnel. Dark broken only by a handheld light. A candle, was it? It's cool in here, a hint of dampness. The lingering smell of…what? Alcohol.

Coarse. Crude. Strong.

Moonshine.

A child then. No. Two children. A boy watching. Another swaddled and cooing.

Then—

Beluga's head snapped back against the car seat, but she never opened her eyes or released her touch on the bottle. Time passed.

A man flips on a light and steps into the tunnel. He goes to the next filled slot on the racks, top to bottom, and reaches for a bottle. This bottle. Who is he? The little boy grown up?

Yes. No. Yes. Almost certainly.

A young woman approaches from the trapdoor

entrance. Was she the swaddled baby?

No. No. Maybe? No.

She carries a glass. Encourages him to drink. He refuses. She insists. He sips and hands her back the glass, then returns to the next bottle in the rack.

A large older man appears behind the first man. He has been waiting for this moment. Watching.

She sees him watching, shrugs, and turns to leave.

The older man steps from shadow to light and—

Beluga gasped for air as if she just broke through the surface after a near drowning. Her eyes stared, but they were unseeing. The bottle rolled from her hands and settled between the seats.

Planchette leapt to his feet and nuzzled her under the chin. After no acceptable response he swatted her on the cheek and yowled long and hard. Her eyelids fluttered then, and she weakly extended her hand to pat his body as assurance she would be fine.

Moments passed.

Doc dry swallowed and waited until Beluga sat up a little in the seat. "You scared the hell out of us."

"I'm sorry."

"You should be. You took ten years off my life, ten years I can't afford, and at least one of Planchette's lives."

"I'm sorry. Really."

Doc eyed the bottle with concern, retrieved it carefully as if after all this it would sting him, and settled it back in his lap. "Have I made it clear you scared the hell out of us?"

"Clear as a crystal ball."

He hesitated as if asking the next question might give him an answer he'd rather not know. "So, did you get anything?”

    “Yes.”

    “Anything worthwhile?”

    “I'm afraid so, Doc. Very, very afraid.”

Chapter 18

"Hi, Mom."

"Darling." Beluga grabbed Olivia in a bear hug, rocked her back and forth, eyed the cooking school building profile from a place in the woods near the back parking lot, then whispered in her ear, "All clear? No one else knows we're back?"

"No one."

"Fabulous."

"Unless you count Auntie Tanya."

Beluga took a step back. "You didn't."

"I had to, Mom. She was stuck to me like spandex on a sweaty body."

"And there's the image I really hoped to avoid."

"Did you know she's speaking Greek to everyone?"

"Is anyone answering?"

"No."

"There's a blessing."

Olivia scrutinized her mother. "Are you okay?"

"Nothing that three days sleep and a solid meal wouldn't fix."

"You look awful. And I gotta say you're rather pungent."

"Guano."

"Of course. What else would it be?"

"I can explain, Olivia."

"Please don't."

"But I can."

"And I'm begging you not to. Really. The more I know, the more I'm inclined to follow through with my plan to put you in a home."

"Let's make a date to disagree on that topic another time." Beluga kissed her daughter on the cheek. "Right now we need to get your other plans in motion."

Planchette emerged from the woods and, upon seeing Olivia, picked up his pace and launched himself into her arms. The two nuzzled each other, one purring, the other cooing, then both turned at the same time to watch as Doc approached carrying a wine bottle.

Olivia offered her hand. "Olivia Stein. You must be Doc."

He took her hand and bowed deeply. "I'm positively enchanted. You are a journalist, I understand?"

"Freelance feature writer. A friend got me the job after I got back from doing some volunteer work."

"Ah, yes," Doc said. "Teaching South American children to read. A noble pursuit. But now you find yourself mired in this dilemma."

"I was in the area researching eccentric people and their hobbies—"

"And you never called me?" Beluga said. "I mean, not as an eccentric with a hobby, as fascinating as both of us are I should add, but because I'm your mother and a call wouldn't kill you."

Olivia ignored her. "It was pure coincidence I was up here—"

"There is no coincidence," Beluga said. "Fate maybe. A divine plan perhaps. Even a peculiar alignment of stars and planets. But coincidence? Never."

Olivia took a deep breath, held it, then continued, "Darwin called 911, then he called me. He thought you were dead, Mom. He was frantic. He made me frantic. Everyone was frantic because you were trying to track down a murderer. It was a stupid risk, and you could have been killed."

"But I wasn't killed."

"But you could have been. Even if you did save the life of," Olivia rifled through a notepad, "chef student, Jeannette Regina Mason." She stopped then and brushed away a tear. "Sometimes you make me crazy and I hate you for it, but then you go do something that makes me love you again, and I hate that."

Beluga touched Olivia softly on the cheek. "I love you, too, sweetheart."

"A journalist and a diplomat," Doc said. "I'm honored to finally be in the presence of a woman with such grace and beauty."

Beluga snorted. "You used to say that to me."

"Things change," Doc said. "Especially now that you have coerced me into being a thread in this tangled tapestry of deception."

"You have the wine; you have the knowledge; and you can bullshit with the best of them. Here's hoping Ned Niblett won't have a chance."

"Ah, yes. The plan to engage the renowned head of the cooking school in a discussion of vinifera and their ultimate product. Lead on, young Ms. Stein."

Olivia cleared her throat. "Well, Doc, it's kind of difficult in there right now. Ned Niblett is holed up in his office and won't come out, claiming that something is after him."

"The cluricaun," Beluga said, nodding.

"Whatever."

"No. Really. I can explain that, too."

"Later, if you must. Anyway, the students are gathered in the dining room turning comatose while Chef Pernod reviews the hazards of a commercial kitchen. Mechanical, biological, or viral, the dangers fortunately seem limited, but Chef Pernod's worse case scenarios are anything but limited. She even started in on exploding foods, including an Apricot Brandy Chicken recipe that is known for blowing doors off ovens. And get this, she claims Paul Prudhomme once referred to rue as 'Cajun napalm,' and proceeded to explain why in great detail. Some might even say excruciating detail."

"I'm sorry I missed that," Beluga said. "Did she ever get into the volatility of boiled eggs, or would that be exclusively on a need-to-know?"

"Mother, please." Olivia continued. "Standing in the back of the room are a couple of uniformed police officers who have made a career out of looking at their watches. To kill time as it were."

"What are the police still doing here?" Beluga asked.

"Watching. They've interviewed all the students, but they think there's more than meets the eye."

"Indeed there is," said Beluga.

"Absolutely there is," Olivia said.

Beluga stopped and stared. "You know something."

"Yes, Mom, I do. Whether or not it'll help remains to be seen."

"Spill it, my darling."

"No time. We've got to act while we can. The students can't be held captive forever. So here's the plan I've cooked up."

Three of them leaned into a huddle formation awaiting orders. The fourth member of the group sat on the ground intently watching the others.

"Doc, go to Chef Niblett's office and present the bottle of wine for his consideration and opinion. If there's any shot he'll come out, that's the one reason I'm betting on."

"Check," Doc said.

Beluga nodded. "Yes, he's an expert on wine, and this bottle might just shake a little information out of him as to why he was in Chef Doe's cellar."

Olivia raised an eyebrow. "Clearly you know a little something, too, Mom."

"Whether or not it'll help remains to be seen."

Olivia pointed at Planchette. "You're going to be in charge of causing chaos, bedlam, and anarchy."

"Excellent choice," Beluga said.

"Your motivation, should you choose to accept it, is everyone covered in catnip, and you need a fix right now. Or you can imagine gourmet canned food. Whatever works."

The tip of Planchette's tail twitched. His gaze turned suddenly inward as if contemplating the means to an end.

"And, Mom—"

"Ready and willing, my little love boat."

"Under this plan Chef Niblett should be distracted, the students and officers hopefully will be bumping into each other, and Chef Pernod will simply freak."

"Well spoken my dear."

"That's the sign for Tanya to herd Burton Smith into a room next to the kitchen. When we arrive she'll lock the door, and you can start your interrogation." Olivia stepped back from the huddle then. "That's the best I could come up with on such short notice. If you'd called me from more than a couple of miles from the school, I might have had more."

"A few more miles and you could have had time for the plan to be professionally published and distributed."

"Don't start, Beluga," Doc warned.

Olivia looked at them, then stuck her hand into the middle of the circle. Doc added his hand to hers, followed by Beluga. Planchette curled around Olivia's legs, then stopped for the cue.

"What are we waiting for? Ready? Set? *Go!*"

And they were off.

Doc pulled open the door to the building, waved the rest in, and created a bottleneck of mammalian physical presence when he tried to press through at the same time. "Pardon me's," and "So sorry's" were uttered as they eventually broke the jam and scattered to their respective duties.

Beluga cocked her head toward the administration office and watched as Doc squared his shoulders and proceeded in.

Olivia grabbed her mother's arm and walked slowly behind Planchette, who loped the length of the lobby hallway, and turned the corner to the dining room.

There was an ominous silence at first, and finally came the sounds they were hoping for.

Planchette let loose a shriek in cat-speak.

A female scream came next, followed by the generous use of startled surprise and expletives from many members of those assembled. Books spilled from table tops, chairs were upended, a line of Greek—possibly discussing bus routes—split the air, and the command from Chef Pernod to stay calm in the midst of a biological disaster was completely ignored.

A low rumble and a subtle vibration rippled through the floor.

"Chaos, bedlam, and anarchy." A catch formed in Beluga's throat. "I couldn't be more proud of my boy."

"There's something else, Mom."

"What else?"

The vibration increased so that they could feel it through the soles of their shoes. That could mean only one thing. A mass exodus. Or, as it was in this case—

"Stampede!"

There they came. Dozens of students all turned the corner and approached them at breakneck speed. Vying for position to be at the head of the crowd to get the hell out of there, they threw elbows and oaths, and shouted "Save yourself" with alarming enthusiasm. The running of the bulls in Pamplona suddenly looked like a stroll through a petting zoo.

"We gotta get past them, Mom."

"Are you out of your mind?"

"We have to get to Tanya and your witness while no one's paying attention."

The crowd was upon them then, and pulled them into their midst to be herded unwillingly to the door. It was like swimming against a tsunami, and about as effective.

A backpack swatted Beluga in the head and she reeled. Stars danced in her eyes. "Olivia! Olivia!"

From deep in the mass of humanity came the reply, "Mom! Where are you? Mom!"

"Olivia!" A breath of fresh air touched her then.

The door. Someone had opened the door. But the sheer depth of humanity trying to squeeze into the small opening allowed no one to pass. As one the crowd panicked and pushed harder.

A backpack, another one maybe, it was hard to say, batted her rhythmically until she thought she'd lose consciousness or commit homicide. Frankly, she preferred the latter since right now that would be so much more satisfying.

Something brushed against her, touched her chest, then vanished. The touch returned almost immediately, and with a determined tug got hold of a wad of her muumuu and pulled. She was dragged through the writhing horde and deposited outside the circle of madness where she could finally take a deep breath when the blockage at the door popped and successfully released the first handful of people and dispersed the crowd.

She turned to identify her good Samaritan, and watched as he dug deep into his breast pocket. "Tony?"

Large strands of hair had loosed itself from his ponytail and dropped across his face. He tucked them behind his ear and waved the pack of filterless cigarettes recovered from his pocket. "Never, *never* get in the way of chef students who need a smoke."

"That's what caused the charge?"

He pointed in the general direction of the door.

The entrance was free of people, but just outside

was a healthy percentage of them actively creating a haze of gray-blue smoke. Others stood at the periphery and enjoyed the sunlight, while a few drifted to their cars.

"Great. I think I'll join them."

"Mom." Olivia's voice echoed off the empty halls. There was more than a little annoyance in her voice. "The plan."

Beluga shrugged. "Well, maybe later."

Tony nodded. "We'll be here. Most of us anyway."

"Why?"

"Chef Doe was the best. We want to know who thought otherwise."

"And the others? Why did they leave?"

"Some didn't know him, and some couldn't take another lecture by Chef Pernod. Your cat was the ticket to freedom."

"Any port in a storm."

"Something like that."

She offered her hand and he took it. "Thanks, Tony. I owe you."

"Find the murderer, and I'll owe you." Then he was through the door and enveloped in the cloud of smoke.

Nice guy. An award-winning chef sooner than he would have even hoped. The accolades were coming. No doubt about it. Now if she could train a burst of intuition on the matter at hand, well, that would be something.

"Mom."

"Right behind you." She strode down the hall, picked up the pace to an almost trot, then stopped suddenly and looked at the administration offices where

Ned Niblett lived and through the lobby door where Tony, Katie Cliff, and the other students stood.

If it was a student who killed John Doe, wouldn't he or she take this opportunity to clear out and never come back? Sure. That was possible. But wasn't it also possible that the killer might want to hang around? See what happens? Or see if anything emerges that could point to him or her as the murderer so he, or she, could take action? Yes. That felt right. The hairs on her neck stood up as affirmation of her suspicions.

Yet, the devil and his advocate could say that it was also possible that the murderer could be, at this very moment, out on the loose, or even in the local hospital as the result of a smokehouse accident.

She shook her head as if that would clear the confusion of thoughts that circled and taunted and offered too many possibilities. Still, the fact remained that each and every possibility was viable somehow. One person touched the other, was a part of the other. Somehow....

"*Mom!*"

"Coming, dear." She proceeded down the hall toward Olivia, the dining room, and the now hopefully detained Burton Smith.

Interconnected. All of these people. One to the other. But how?

Who among them was responsible for the ultimate act that ended a person's life?

Soon now. Soon. It would all become clear and then, finally, it would be over.

At least she hoped so.

Chapter 19

It was quiet in the dining room. A little too quiet if anyone bothered to ask for an opinion. But no one did.

That included Chef Pernod who stood still in front of a sea of dining room chairs facing her in the aftermath of a lecture gone horribly awry. Her face flashed a myriad of emotions, one after another, like a silent film shown on an erratic, antique projector. Was she puzzled? Probably. A bit mystified? Okay. Anxious and maybe frightened? Yes and yes.

The chef glanced at the black cat that stood at her feet and swatted her in a menacing manner every time she made the slightest move to take an exit step. Whether it was the mass exodus during a riveting lecture topic that caused her confusion, the very idea that cooking classes had been suspended because of murder, a murder itself and in a commercial freezer at that, or that a cat was now calling the shots in a professional dining room—a clear health code violation, the chef would argue—was anyone's guess.

So the chef settled on the one thing she did best and gave her the most comfort; she continued the lecture. From the vacancy in her eyes, it didn't matter that no one was there to listen. What mattered was she retained some semblance of personal control when all about her others had clearly lost theirs. She dry swallowed, paused briefly after a cursory glance at the renegade cat, then continued to talk. And never once did she exhibit a hint of acknowledgement at Beluga and Olivia's arrival, or their equally quick disappearance into one of the side meeting rooms.

"I fear for her sanity," Olivia whispered.

"Apparently a lack of sanity is par for the course for cooking professionals. I mean, no sane person would voluntarily stand for hours at a time in sweltering heat, hip to hip amid other like-minded people, for the sake of turning out a series of complex dishes that look like they just whipped them up. But speaking of questionable sanity…"

"Auntie Tanya," Olivia said, taking in the scene that played in the middle of the room. "What are you doing?"

Burton Smith sat sullen in a chair while Tanya held a lone light bulb, unconnected by wire or fixture, over his head. "*Pos tha pliroforiso tin astinomia yi afto*? How do I inform the police about this?"

Beluga waved toward the door. "I'm thinking a quick call to the smoking section ought to bring them running. If not for definitive police action, they might at least get a good laugh when they see this."

"The use of a lone bulb is a standard police interrogation tactic," Tanya said imperiously.

"If you're in a bad movie that doesn't bother to let facts stand in the way," Olivia said.

Beluga nodded. "Or electricity. The bulb is supposed to be lit, my dear."

"Oh." Tanya lowered the bulb and stared at her victim. "I guess I didn't think it through. But he looks cowed enough. Something in my plan had him worried."

"I daresay that's true enough. Your plans always worry me. But let's see if Mr. Smith might be amenable to a different approach." Beluga pulled up a chair to sit next to the man. "What do you say, Burton? Are you game for helping us out if I insist Tanya review the Geneva Conventions?"

He considered this request carefully and formed a question of his own. "And if I don't?"

"We have no authority, no way to hold you against your will, and no credentials—save for bad student photo IDs—that can in anyway mandate your cooperation."

"Damn tootin'."

"But I sure would appreciate a break in this case. I'm thinking you may be the one who can help us out."

Burton Smith eyed Tanya with deep suspicion. "What did you have in mind?"

Tanya winked. "A date."

"A few questions," Olivia said, stepping between Tanya and Burton.

"You go first, Mom."

"There's a connection here. Between the students, the chef, a few odd visions and feelings that came to me over a bottle of wine—you know, the usual—but I can't quite make it all fit."

Burton shifted uncomfortably in his chair. "You know about the wine?"

"Held a bottle in my very hands."

"And the tunnel-turned-cellar?"

"Yes," Beluga said, squirming as if still dropped in the hole that led to the discovery. "Rather intimately."

"Okay then. Good." The man relaxed a notch. "That was some of my best work, that cellar."

"So feel free to talk openly. There's probably nothing you can say that will catch me off guard."

"Then you know the tunnel was once the hiding place for a still."

"Yep. Saw the evidence with my very own eyes."

"Then you know about the inheritance fight, too. Ugly business that." He sighed deeply and offered a small, relieved smile. "At least it's out in the open now."

"Say again?"

"Ugly business. But not as ugly as the ongoing feud with Ned Niblett. Say, getting this off my chest feels pretty darned good."

"Whoa there, cowboy. I think we've come across some undiscovered territory, and we need to circle the wagons."

Tanya's eyes popped open to full alert. "He's a cowboy, too? What kind of admission credentials does this place demand?"

"Clearly not stringent enough to keep some out," Beluga droned. "It was a figure of speech, dear heart."

"Damn." Tanya sighed heavily and looked over Olivia's shoulder. "I've always loved a frontier man."

"Auntie Tanya, please."

"I'm just saying."

"Zip it, Tanya." Beluga inched her chair closer to Burton Smith. "Let's take this a step at a time, if you don't mind." She cleared her throat, thought about a delicate approach, shrugged, then called it as it came to her. "Inheritance fight? Do elaborate and don't skimp on details."

"Well," Burton Smith said with some hesitancy. "I guess it don't matter much now who knows since everyone's about to find out soon enough, what with the chef being dead and all."

"Oooh," Tanya said, draping an arm over Olivia's shoulder. "Don't you just love how these frontier men speak? You know, if I wasn't wearing support hose my knees might have positively buckled."

"God forbid the stomach panel in those hose go, too. There wouldn't be a single witness left from the impact."

Burton Smith glanced from one to another, then appeared to swallow with some difficulty.

"You are a hateful woman, Beluga Stein," Tanya said.

"I'm on a mission, and you're distracting me."

Olivia rose to the cause. "Mr. Smith, please forgive these two. They've known each other since kindergarten and still think they're fighting over who got the best snack before nap time. You were saying everyone's going to find out soon anyway? Find out what?"

"About the money. You know, from the wine."

"Yes," Beluga said, returning to the conversation. "There does seem to be a great deal of value tied up in those bottles." She caught the questioning look in Olivia's eyes. "So I've been told. My knowledge is pretty well limited to red, white, and a few shades in-between."

"The damned thing about it is," Burton said, shaking his head, "the chef didn't drink."

"Not a drop?"

"A teetotaler he was."

"Chef Doe?"

"Couldn't stand the stuff. It seems alcohol in one

form or another ran in the family, and so did a problem with over-consumption, if you get my drift. The still belonged to Chef Doe's grandfather, and the wine belonged to his father. The father never told anyone about his collection, including his kids, since the three never got along too good. Turns out he had a bit of a gambling problem along with the drinking one. The gambling, in wine anyway, paid off handsomely, or would have if he'd lived long enough to sell what he didn't drink."

"So Chef Doe never knew about the wine until he moved into the house and discovered the tunnel?"

"He sure knew what it was worth when he found it. So did Ned Niblett. That's when the problems started."

"Problems? As in the plural of problem?"

"Yessim. Every week, like clockwork, the chef—Chef Doe, that is—would bring in one of those fancy bottles to school, and it would disappear. Just like that. No one saw a thing. Then the chef—Chef Niblett, that is—would get himself all in a knot and there'd be a fight between the two."

"Fisticuffs?" Tanya asked in amazement.

"No, not like that. Verbal meanness, a little cussedness. Some threats. They didn't think we knew, but we did. All of us. It's a small world around here, and news travels pretty fast."

"Especially interesting news, I suppose." And especially if a teetotaler had access to fine wine, very fine wine, and a master chef with credentials in spirits was left out of the loop.

Spirits.

Hmm. A hint of something else, yet another connection, touched the periphery of Beluga's mind, then skittered away. She fought to get the thought back…Spirits. Ghosts. Apparitions. Specters. Other beings, like say……cluricauns.

Could it be? Was there something connected between Ned Niblett's cluricaun buddy and the late, fascinating newly complex Chef Doe? And could it mean a motive for murder by none other than the head of the cooking school? Hmm. Problem was, it didn't all add up quite right.

"Burton," Beluga said, staring right into the man's eyes, "Ned Niblett can't be part of this inheritance issue. I mean, that doesn't make sense, not even in the most remote of familial conditions. Besides, you referred to it as an inheritance fight which—correct me if I'm wrong—implies a more immediate state of mind with all interested parties weighing in."

"I wouldn't know about—"

"So, that can only mean one thing, or rather, one person."

"Who, Mom?"

"Jeannette Regina Mason. AKA Jackleg."

"The woman you sent to the hospital?"

"Yeah. Inherent in that is a problem, since I'm here and she's there. Probably heavily sedated."

Tanya swooned. "Lucky girl."

"For your information, Olivia, I didn't send her to the hospital; her injuries did. Let's get that perfectly clear right now, shall we?"

"Jeannette Mason was in an inheritance fight with Chef Doe?"

"She is his sister, after all." Beluga caught the questioning look in Olivia's eyes. "So I've been told. But what would they be fighting over? His wine collection?"

"His land."

All turned to Burton Smith.

He nodded at their surprise. "Yep. He had loads of it. Acres and acres of prime countryside. Left to him by his daddy."

"Left only to him?" Beluga asked. "Was Jeannette cut out of the will?"

Burton Smith stroked his chin. "I'm thinking she had the lower section. Just as nice, mind you, pretty as a picture. But seeing as how she had no plans to live here, there was no need for her to have the house."

"And the tunnel," Olivia added.

"With the wine," Beluga said. "Does that mean she didn't know about the wine and so the value which went with the house?"

"I don't think she knew," Burton said, "I think she does now, though how I couldn't say. I'd just be passing on rumor and speculation."

Tanya nodded and tossed out a comment. "Like everyone else in this town. They say the same thing."

Mother and daughter whirled toward Tanya.

Beluga got the words out first. "How do you know that?"

"What? Did you think I was just going to sit around and do nothing while you were cavorting about? I have a few investigative skills of my own, you know." She examined her talon-like fingernails, then scraped one against the side of an incisor. "I like to keep busy. Sue me."

"Maybe later. It depends on what you found out."

Tanya glowed in the sudden spotlight. "Perhaps it's my womanly charms, or maybe it's my ability to talk to anyone of any station at anytime of the day or—"

"Get to it, Tanya. While I'm still breathing and vibrant, if you don't mind."

"Honestly, you are so impatient."

"The root of homicide, my dear. At least with my current thinking."

"Well, you're not alone in that thinking."

"Impatience as the root of homicide?"

"Exactly."

"Tanya, please. Get to the point or suffer the consequences of a weak blood vessel exploding in my head, which means it'll be on your head."

Tanya seemed puzzled for a moment, but regained herself quickly. "The rumor varied on some points, but they all held a common thread. Jeannette Mason got her inheritance land and didn't mind the chef getting the house. It was about to fall apart anyway."

"Yep," Burton agreed. "That much is true. That's why I was called in to fix up the place, along with the cellar. The chef got the teaching job here and needed a place to live. Fixing the cabin up was cheaper than buying a new place."

"You had your time, frontier man." Tanya shooed him off the chair and sat down when it was vacated. "It's my turn to talk now."

Beluga's patience was wearing thin. "Then talk, Tanya. And be quick about it."

"Their father moved here after a nasty divorce when the kids were little, so neither one of them had a stake in the place, so to speak. The story is Jeannette planned to sell her share of the land to help finance her education, but then suddenly, without anyone knowing why, she showed up at the very cooking school where her brother was an instructor."

"That seems odd," Olivia said. "Wouldn't that be against the rules?"

"Not necessarily," said Beluga. "Unless she took a class that her brother taught."

"That's likely, with the way the curriculum is set up."

"And as short-handed as they are around here…" Beluga thought a moment. "Maybe Chef Niblett didn't know about the family ties, and Jeannette kinda came in without anyone noticing."

Burton Smith cleared his throat. "He knew about her. Yes, indeed. He knew all about her."

"Did he." It was a statement rather than a question because the vision Beluga had while holding the bottle of wine suddenly returned to her full force. "Chef Doe knew about the tunnel and the wine a long time ago because he was there. He was a child, mind you, so maybe his memories were a little foggy, but an underground tunnel is something you don't forget. Jackleg, er, Jeannette, was just a baby. She wouldn't remember a thing. So someone had to have told her. I think I know who that someone is."

"Who?" Tanya asked impatiently.

Just as important, Beluga suddenly realized, was the identity of the young woman who stood in the tunnel and encouraged Chef Doe to drink. He had refused, but she had insisted, and so he drank. It was the last drink he would ever take.

Beluga dreaded the idea that what she suspected might actually be the truth. "Damn it."

"What?" Tanya asked.

"What is it, Mom?"

"Sometimes I hate it when I'm right." But there was no time to dwell on personal kudos.

A scream exploded from the kitchen. Long and loud, definitely female. It echoed off tile walls and floors and threatened to puncture eardrums and make squinting a permanent facial expression.

Beluga took a deep breath, shored herself for the worse, and stepped toward the kitchen with every nerve on red alert. "Fasten your seatbelts, folks. We're in for a wild ride."

Chapter 20

The screaming stopped almost as suddenly as it started.

Beluga arrived first at the student lockers near the kitchen office by way of the back hallway. She was followed too closely by Olivia, Tanya, then Burton Smith. The domino effect hit full force when Beluga abruptly halted to survey what she could see of the ware washing area and the corner of what appeared to be an empty kitchen. The back up three promptly pummeled into her from behind and knocked her off her feet. She landed in a heap on the floor and forced the others to join her in the collective collapse.

Planchette appeared in the blink of an eye and used the mountain of humanity as a springboard to land in front of them. His ears sat low on his head and a growl came from deep in his throat while he surveyed the place without benefit of blinking.

"Well, that was fun." Tanya said, pulling herself off Burton more slowly than was necessary. "We should do that again sometime. But maybe with whipped cream as an added incentive."

"What is it, boy?" Beluga asked of her familiar. "Do you see her anywhere?"

"Who, Mom?" Olivia sprang to her feet like a gymnast preparing for a gold medal. "Who do you expect to see?"

"Katie Cliff. It had to be her. I'd recognize that brown-nose tone anywhere, even if it was under a calculated scream."

Olivia tugged her mother up to stand. "The scream was fake?"

"Sounded real enough to me," Burton Smith said, standing and stepping a safe distance away from Tanya.

"Ah, but it was a ruse," Beluga said, looking from Planchette to where the corner of the kitchen began and back to her cat. "She went from the smoking area to the kitchen and let loose a scream ruse. Meant to get us in here in a hurry—"

Tanya snorted. "It worked. And can I just say my kneecaps will never be the same?"

"But where is she?"

The sound of a lock being thrown forced them to look back from whence they came.

The sound of a voice turned them toward the kitchen to get a visual on the source.

"Finally," the voice said.

It was female. Curt. All business. Far from brown-nosing this time, she preferred a threatening tone instead.

Katie Cliff strolled into view. Her face showed a hardness that belied her youth and, until this moment, a practiced act of naiveté. "Now it ends."

Then there was another sound, one that Beluga had heard all too often and under very different circumstances. The hair rose on her arms and a cold shiver danced across her neck and down her spine. She trembled. A knot formed in her stomach and forced her to the unfamiliar brink of tears.

"No. There's no reason he should be here. He's an

innocent."

"He's yours. That's reason enough I brought him here. I always do my homework."

Beluga charged Katie, but she was too quick. In an instant the girl was deep inside the kitchen and held a knife to Emerson's throat.

Emerson's eyes widened. He tried to pull away, but the rope around his neck was tightly connected to the legs of a stainless steel table. Watching his mistress with confusion and fear, he whimpered a little goat-speak, then stood still.

Beluga tried to make her voice calm and soothing. "It'll be okay, honey. It'll be fine."

"Will it?" Katie said, gesturing with the knife. She glared suddenly at the others who had stepped fully into the kitchen. "Stay back, or the goat gets it."

"What do you want?" Beluga asked, her voice cracking and high with anxiety.

"I want you to quit snooping around. I want you to leave and never mention a word to anyone about anything you think you know."

"You'll let Emerson go then?"

"Maybe. Although, this is a cooking school, and I'm guessing there's plenty of things we could do with a goat."

Tanya gasped. "You wouldn't."

Katie offered a tight smile. "After attempting murder on people, do you think I'd hesitate over this? Besides," she said, addressing Beluga, "I don't know that I could trust you from meddling in one form or another, now that I think about it. So let's just say your goat and I will be inseparable for a long time to come."

Attempted murder? Or was it more than that, like,

say, full-blown murder? Katie was no doubt the woman in Beluga's vision. The very one who forced Chef Doe into the depths of the tunnel and wine cellar, to take a drink containing the poisonous Lily of the Valley. The chef was now most decidedly dead, but was he killed after that first drink? Or was he merely incapacitated until he could be permanently taken out of the picture? Suddenly Beluga couldn't be sure.

Speaking of drinks, Beluga realized Katie was the very one who delivered the Dromedary Spits to Jackleg. She shuddered. One had even been delivered to herself. Sure, Tanya supposedly made the drinks, but the garnish added to the drinks might have come from assistant bartender Katie. That was possible, wasn't it?

Jackleg recognized the garnish, or did she? She was, after all, a student herself and could have missed something. She could have overlooked something... poisonous. But Jackleg was alive. Maybe not alive and well, but she was alive, and Lily of the Valley was pretty serious business. Still, something had to have been added to the cocktail that would render Jackleg pliable enough to be hauled away to a smokehouse and hung from meat hooks.

This theory brought her to the next thought: the pulley system. Physics and Doc's explanation proved that even someone as slight as Katie could have done it. Jackleg was impaired, but maybe not so impaired that she could still be guided to a waiting car, driven out to the chef's house, walked through the tunnel, and connected to hooks. Then even petite Katie could hoist Jackleg up in the air and leave her.

For dead.

Attempted murder on both counts? For sure. Actual

murder? Maybe one at least. But the motive for such acts remained unclear. Beluga needed more information, and she needed a way to get it efficiently. White lies were sometimes helpful in these matters, but desperate times called for whoppers.

"Suppose I could get you off from the attempted murder thing?"

Something fleeting, hesitant, crossed Katie's face, then disappeared again. "No. It's not possible. It's all too complicated now."

"It was Lily of the Valley in the drink that killed Chef Doe, wasn't it? But did you make it? Plan for it?"

Katie seemed suddenly bewildered.

"There was something else in Jackleg's drink. What was it, Katie? What did you put in that drink?"

Doc's voice pierced the air. "*Solanum tuberoscum.*"

From the back hallway, where they had heard a lock being thrown, came Doc escorted by Ned Niblett. Or rather, Doc was being held tightly around the upper chest and guided slowly into the kitchen by Ned Niblett.

"Mom!" Olivia gasped. "The chef has a knife under Doc's chin!" She gasped again. "With the other hand he's holding Doc *and* a wine bottle."

"I guess that's what comes from years of experience juggling things in the kitchen," Beluga squeaked. "Are you okay, Doc?"

"I've been better."

"What is with the knife thing around here?" Tanya asked.

Doc rolled his eyes at her. "Oh, I don't know. Maybe because there's a lot of them around?"

"That's enough," Ned Niblett said.

Doc continued anyway. "Some, I've come to find out, are highly specialized and quite expensive, not to mention sharp. Take this one for instance." Doc pointed at the implement held at his throat and revealed a clean, bleeding laceration on the palm of his hand. "And the damn thing about it is that my injury came from touching the *back* of the blade."

Ned Niblett's eyes glittered. "The blade is even sharper. I know. I'm a professional."

"Oh, my." Tanya looked closely around the kitchen for the first time and saw what appeared to be an impressive arsenal of potential murder utensils. Her gaze settled on a large, flat slotted spoon, her hand went to her throat, and her voice turned weak and thin. "I think this is all a little too much for me. I'll catch you later." In slow motion, her knees weakened, buckled, and she dropped face forward onto the floor with an audible thud.

"Who is that woman?" asked Ned Niblett.

"A safety and sanitation student," said Beluga.

"Well," he said, "that explains it. Leave her." He tightened his hold on Doc and turned to Beluga. "What remains unexplained is why you're still here." Beluga opened her mouth to answer, but Ned Niblett cut her off. "No matter. There's enough soup left to keep everyone quiet. Unfortunately it was made by a student who mistook a rather lethal ingredient for wild garlic."

Doc nodded ever so slightly. "Lily of the Valley."

"I didn't make the soup," Katie said.

Ned Niblett gave her a withering look, and she fell silent. "A professional chef gathered the ingredients from his own garden—"

The haphazardly buried plant in Chef Doe's herb garden, Beluga knew then. Niblett was trying to set up the scenario for an accidental poisoning instead of what was an obvious murder.

"—and the student followed the recipe given to her. Unfortunate circumstances and even more unfortunate in the outcome, no doubt about it, but this situation is not without precedent."

"*Solanum tuberoscum*," Beluga said suddenly. "That's not Lily of the Valley, but that's what was in Jackleg's drink." She hoped the look on her face was one of knowledge and deep intellectual insight punctuated by a touch of admiration to a healthy egotist for such a well-laid plan. In truth, she didn't have a clue what she was talking about, and even less idea what the sola-tuberscam, or whatever it was, was. But since ignorance was supposedly bliss, she ought to be nearing nirvana anytime now.

Ned Niblett shrugged. "A simple garnish. But effective if played right."

Katie's voice turned suddenly soft and introspective. "Played right? What do you mean?"

"Not now," Niblett said.

Katie shook her head. "I don't understand. What do you mean 'played right?'"

"I said, *not now*."

The young woman looked at Beluga. "What does he mean? Do you understand what he's talking about?"

Sadly, Beluga did. It was clear now more than ever. The enthusiastically competitive Katie Cliff did whatever it took to win the approval and a few extra points from the well-renowned chef and head of the cooking school. A recipe here, a passing comment or book opened to reveal a special culinary touch to make a student stand out as exemplary, like, say, offering a poisonous drink, or a toxic garnish to a drink, and Katie was as special as she wanted to be. She was played all right. But she wasn't without malice herself.

"You gave Chef Doe something to drink in the wine cellar."

"Yes," Katie said with some hesitancy. "But he barely touched it."

"It was enough to make him ill. Then you brought him back here and gave him soup."

"But I didn't make the soup."

Ned Niblett glared at her. "Enough, young lady."

Katie turned to the chef. "You made the soup."

"*Quiet!*"

"You said it was his favorite. You said if I gave it to him he would like me better than her."

"Her?" Beluga asked. "Who's her?"

"Jackleg. Jeannette Mason. She tried to take him away from me, but I was his girlfriend. Not her."

"Girlfriend?" Beluga shook her head. "No, Katie. Jackleg is Chef Doe's sister, not his love interest. Although I can understand your mistake, since, well, er, others might have assumed the same thing."

"She's not his...?" Katie looked at Ned Niblett. "But you told me..."

"What did I tell you, young lady? What exactly did I tell you?"

"That she killed Chef Doe."

"That may be what you heard, Miss Cliff. But that's not what I said. I said she was here to protect what was rightfully hers, whatever it took. You filled in the blanks."

"No. That's not right." She gazed wildly about the room. "That's not right."

Beluga edged closer to Katie and Emerson. Her voice softened. "You thought she killed Chef Doe with poisonous soup, so you decided to kill her."

"I was going to teach her a lesson, that's all."

"Hoisted up on a meat hook in an abandoned smokehouse?" Doc said. "That's some lesson. I know I'd never forget it."

Katie pointed at Ned Niblett with the knife. "He told me how to make the soup. About a sprout that could be used in a salad. Or as a garnish in a drink."

"Once again you are mistaken, Miss Cliff."

"The picture of the pretty garnish that can make you sleepy? You showed me that."

Doc piped in, "Actually it can induce coma, but who's counting."

"The picture was on a table top, Miss Cliff. Anyone could have seen it."

"You showed me the smokehouse and the thing that hangs meat."

"An instructional opportunity for an eager student. Nothing more."

Katie froze in place for a second. Two. Her voice turned cold. "You played me, Chef. You killed Chef Doe, and you played me to do the rest."

"You were a willing participant."

"You played me for the wine. For the wine and because you were jealous of Chef Doe."

"Petty emotions like jealousy bore me, Miss Cliff."

It hit Beluga then. It hit her like a brick through a weak window. She stepped to within touching distance of Katie Cliff and turned to Ned Niblett. "You knew

John Doe from before, didn't you?"

"I do not recall such an encounter, Ms. Stein."

"He was fired by Chef Niblett," Katie said. "A long time ago. Chef Niblett had a restaurant, and he was threatened by any talented cooks who came along."

"That's true," Burton Smith added. "The chef— Chef Doe, that is—told me the same thing. He was none too happy about Chef Niblett's arrival at the school here, or that the chef—Chef Niblett again— talked Ms. Jackleg into quitting the CIA to come here to finish school."

Beluga stared at Ned Niblett. "You brought Jackleg, er, Jeannette Mason here?" A slight movement, barely a shadow, in the far corner of the kitchen near the walk-in freezer caught her eye. "You brought her here because…"

Her gaze wandered to the glass window that separated the kitchen from the dining room. Behind the glass stood the sated smokers among the student body, and what appeared to be a shell-shocked Anise Pernod. All watched with great attention, but remained unseen by Ned Niblett, Katie Cliff, and the shadow in the far corner of the room that was becoming more visible with every passing second.

"You brought her here because you were threatened by the students' admiration of Chef Doe, your fear he might take your job, and how he chose to dispose of his wine collection."

"Ms. Stein, I suggested she might want to come here to protect what was rightfully hers. Now it is you filling in the blanks."

"She didn't know about the wine, and the money tied up in those bottles. But you did." Beluga inched closer to the rope that held Emerson. "You killed a beloved cooking instructor just for a regular taste of good hooch?"

"Hooch?" Doc said. "Good God, woman. Have you no respect?"

Ned Niblett eyed Beluga. "Be careful of that which you have no knowledge."

"Like cluricauns?" Beluga said.

Then it happened.

Beluga lunged for Emerson, but Katie's instincts and youth won out.

Against all known physical laws, the cluricaun jumped the space of the kitchen and grabbed for the wine bottle. But this time Neb Niblett's experience won out.

Niblett held the knife point closer to Doc's throat while Katie did the same to the hapless and frightened Emerson. "Choose," Niblett and Katie said at the same time, then stared at each other in surprise.

"I know you can do it," Niblett said to Beluga, while watching the cluricaun circle the kitchen. "I know your reputation. Get rid of my supernatural nemesis and get out of this town, or your friend will regret it."

Katie piped up then. "No. You have to get the chef on murder and get me off, or your goat gets it."

"Choose," they both said again.

Death had touched this place enough. Now it was time for it all to end. Beluga thought deep and hard and sent her psychic messages as best she could. But would they get those messages and understand her plan? She could only hope so, since there was no other way out she could see. Focus. Concentrate. Send.

Message received.

At least she thought it was received. Okay then. Here's hoping for the best. She released a held breath as her gaze went from Doc to Emerson, back again to Doc, and then back to linger on Emerson and the cluricaun who stood just behind.

"You're going to pick the goat?" Doc asked, horrified.

Beluga offered an embarrassed shrug.

"So be it," Ned Niblett said.

"*Now,*" she bellowed.

Suddenly all hell broke loose.

Planchette became airborne with all claws unsheathed. Looking more than twice his size, he landed with centuries of feline anger, experience, and deftness on the back of Ned Niblett's neck and put his razor-sharp weapons to good use.

The cluricaun leapt onto the back of Emerson, snatched the rope free from the table, knocked the knife out of Katie Cliff's hands, and rode the poor goat like they were in a rodeo bucking competition.

Katie's screams were real this time, as was Ned Niblett's, who let Doc loose to fight his new nemesis.

Tanya rallied briefly in time to see the cluricaun ride Emerson within a hair's breadth of her. "No. Not yet," she said weakly and slumped back into her faint.

Emerson had reached his limit. He rose into the air, twisting and turning, bolted forward, then abruptly stopped. The cluricaun flew off the goat's back toward Ned Niblett, stretched an arm out to snatch away the wine bottle, but missed his mark and landed solidly against a locker in the back hall.

Ned Niblett released the bottle of wine to swat at Planchette, and Doc dived for the save. He caught it inches from the tiled floor, then tossed the bottle to Beluga who caught it over her head, but not before it met something solid and unyielding. Katie Cliff went down like a stone and without the slightest sound.

But hell had no fury like a cluricaun scorned. The little supernatural being slammed his fist on the locker which popped open and spilled wilted Lily of the Valley, sprouting potatoes, and a very tall toque, then turned his angry, glittering eyes on Beluga and the bottle in her hand.

"Enough!" Beluga shouted. "Stop it now."

Planchette retracted his claws and jumped to the ground, keeping a watchful eye on both the cluricaun and Ned Niblett.

The chef mopped the rivulets of blood that oozed from many scratches and glared at her. "You'll never pin this on me."

"Oh, but I will," Beluga said, waving expansively at the people behind the glass window. "We all will."

"I heard every word." Burton Smith tied the chef's hands with cheesecloth. "Every one of 'em."

"If all that's not enough," Beluga said, tossing the wine bottle to the cluricaun, "the name on that locker is clearly yours."

The cluricaun tapped the wine bottle against a corner of the wall, and broke off the top.

"Happy now?" she asked.

The little supernatural being raised the bottle in a toast, then drank.

"Me, too."

Chapter 21

Beluga Stein's Diary

All's well that ends well.
At least for some.
It took a while, as it often does, for toxicology reports, but Darwin came through. He is a fine young man, and persistent to boot, and one day he will be an even finer ME, although one hopes he won't develop the unfortunate disposition of his father—the old goat— whom I miss terribly and still have wanton dreams about...
But I digress.
The toxicology report proved the death of Chef Doe was indeed the result of Lily of the Valley. Further official investigations proved it was the hand of Ned Niblett who administered the lethal dose.
Alas, poor Katie Cliff. I didn't know her well, but it turns out she was the cook for the potion and the very one who slipped Jackleg, aka Jeannette Regina Mason, the Solanum tuberoscum in the Dromedary Spits. The solan—thing, by the way, is a potato. Go figure that such a basic staple in kitchens all over the world has poison in the green parts of the plant, the berries, and the sprouts of an unripe potato. The poison is pretty quick, but lucky for Jackleg she didn't get a lot, and she was as healthy as a horse to begin with. If attitude had

anything to do with it she probably wouldn't have felt a thing.

Needless to say, if Ned Niblett or Katie Cliff ever cook again it will be in the confines of a security institution. And since there has been no sign of the cluricaun after Chef Niblett's departure, one presumes the supernatural entity escorted the chef along with the authorities. With or without handcuffs, it's hard to say.

Speaking of goats, and I was just moments ago, my dear, sweet Emerson is back home. No doubt he's even now standing atop his goat house while carefully plotting how to permanently alter my footwear and any other items of clothing he can get his hooves on. But I don't begrudge him his little proclivities after the ordeal he's been through. In fact, I'm so happy to have him safe and sound I might just let him loose in my closet for a free for all. God knows Tanya would be happy to hear that I was considering a redo of my attire. Especially if that meant no more chef jackets and herringbone trousers, which it does. In spades.

That's right. The cooking life is not for me. It wasn't just the murder and attempted murders that clarified this issue for me, although death certainly gives one pause. No. I'm much better suited to the eating life. And if I don't put away this diary, I might miss one of the best repasts of my life.

****

"Beluga, dear, if you don't want your plate you can just pass it over to me." Tanya was dressed for a formal occasion, which in some respects it was. Still, her dress couldn't have been more red, or more tight, or more revealing. "The first, second and third courses were simply divine, but I find it has all made me even more hungry for what's to come."

Beluga nodded. "The students have done a terrific job, haven't they? The dining room here is now one of the best in the county."

Doc snorted and tucked a linen napkin under his bright pink cummerbund. "No doubt about it since about all you can get everywhere else is fatty barbecue, soggy rolls and mushy vegetables." He held up a spear of asparagus as an example. "Look at this, will you? A perfect specimen of *Asparagus officinalis* if ever there was one. Ironic that it's part of the lily family, huh?"

Tanya and Beluga dropped their forks.

"Suit yourself," he said, spearing a vegetable from Beluga's plate. "That means there's more for me." He dragged the asparagus through sauce. "The Hollandaise is perfect. Absolutely perfect."

Beluga eyed her steak *au poivre* with peppercorn brandy cream sauce, and shrugged. "What the hey. With Anise Pernod in charge of the school, everything will be by the book from now on."

"Yeah," Tanya said. "Safety is number one, that's for sure. So if she sees you passing beef bits to Planchette under the table, there'll be hell to pay. Or you'll have to take her class. Or he'll have to take her class. Whichever is worse."

Tony emerged from the kitchen then. He looked as handsome as ever, and set quite a picture as the up-and-coming professional chef in his jacket and toque. He pulled up a chair next to Beluga and eyed her plate. "Not too fond of the asparagus?"

"A little too much family connection, if you get my drift."

He looked at her with the usual mixture of

confusion and pity, but she was used to it.

"Never mind, my dear boy. It's all splendid. A veritable feast for the eyes and stomach."

"Good," he said as he waved to the kitchen. "There's more."

Tanya clapped her hands. "More? Bring it on."

"More?" Beluga said. "I can't eat another bite."

Doc hesitated a moment. "I'll give it a go."

Jeannette "Jackleg" Mason came through the swinging doors, followed by Burton Smith and a host of other students. Each bore their own platter of elaborate and beautifully displayed desserts.

"This isn't part of the planned menu," Jeannette said, "but we wanted to do it anyway. For you."

Beluga looked over the many silver plates of desserts that surrounded her and suddenly felt overwhelmed. Not for the variety of choices, although that was certainly impressive, but at the outpouring of kindness.

"And I didn't think any of you liked me."

"We didn't," the young woman said simply.

"Oh."

"But things change. Thank you, Beluga Stein. Thank you for all you've done."

"My pleasure, Jack, er, Jeannette."

Tony winked at Beluga. "If I ever open my own restaurant, I hope you'll be the first customer."

"Count on it."

Burton Smith offered his dessert to Tanya.

"For me?" she cooed.

"Yessim. You might notice it has lots of whipped cream."

"See?" Tanya said to her tablemates. "They all

come around. Eventually."

The sound of someone clearing her throat parted the dessert parade.

With disapproval etched deeply in her face, Anise Pernod approached the edge of the table. "Do you have an animal in my dining room?"

"It depends on what you mean by animal," Beluga said.

"A cat."

Beluga shrugged. "Kinda."

Chef Pernod snapped her fingers and brought forth a student with a small plate. On it was a fresh piece of salmon, no sauce, no seasoning, and thankfully, no garnish.

"This is for him."

"Really? You mean it?"

"Of course we'll scrub down every inch of this dining room when the two of you vacate, and you'll promise never to bring him back again."

"I promise."

She held up her hand. "Wait. There's more."

"Okay."

"You'll promise never to step into the culinary arts world again."

"Count on it, Chef. It's far too dangerous for me."

Chef Pernod offered the first smile Beluga had ever seen. Maybe the first smile she had ever tried.

"You should consider another field, one a little safer. Like, say, bungee-jumping or hang gliding."

Tanya slapped her hand on the table. Flatware jumped and glasses shook. She wagged a finger at Beluga. "I told you we should do those things. But do you ever listen to me? Nooooo."

"For good reason."

"Just once in your life—"

"Over my dead body."

"The time is never right with you."

"If you're talking about wearing clothes that look like they've been painted on, you said it all. The time is never right."

"Beluga Stein, you take that back."

"Make me."

"I can do it."

"I wish you would."

Their banter started and no matter what anyone said, nothing was going to stop them.

A word about the author...

Wendy W. Webb has published dark fantasy short stories, supernatural-humor murder mystery novels, and stage plays for adults and children.

She's discovered that writing scary stuff and funny stuff is a great excuse to avoid vacuuming, phone scams, and losing precious minutes of her life waiting for someone to back their truck into a parking spot.

She loves animals, Bordeaux wine, theatre, and traveling.

****

www.WendyWebbWriting.com

****

If you enjoyed this story, leaving a review at your favorite book retailer or reader website would be much appreciated. Thank you!

Thank you for purchasing
this publication of The Wild Rose Press, Inc.

For questions or more information
contact us at
info@thewildrosepress.com.

The Wild Rose Press, Inc.
www.thewildrosepress.com